The Mystery in the Old Mine

As Frank led the way out of the mine tunnel, Joe spied a small beam of light at the end. He'd be glad to get some fresh air. Just then, one of the beams overhead creaked ominously.

"What was that?" Frank called out. He shined his flashlight along the ceiling of the shaft. The beam that had made the noise was perilously close to splintering apart.

"Hurry, Joe!" Frank called out. The beam was between Joe and Frank. Joe leaped out of the way just as huge clumps of coal started to fall from above.

"Grab my hand!" Frank shouted desperately, groping for his brother through the downpour of black debris.

But it was too late. The beam broke apart, and the ceiling gave way entirely. More coal came falling from above, and the walls started caving in, too.

Joe Hardy was about to be buried alive!

The Hardy Boys Mystery Stories

#59	Night of the Werewolf
#60	Mystery of the Samurai Sword
#61	The Pentagon Spy
#62	The Apeman's Secret
#63	The Mummy Case
#64	Mystery of Smugglers Cove
#65	The Stone Idol
#66	The Vanishing Thieves
#67	The Outlaw's Silver
#68	Deadly Chase
#69	The Four-headed Dragon
#70	The Infinity Clue
#71	Track of the Zombie
#72	The Voodoo Plot
#73	The Billion Dollar Ransom
#74	Tic-Tac-Terror
#75	Trapped at Sea
#76	Game Plan for Disaster
#77	The Crimson Flame
#78	Cave-in!
#79	Sky Sabotage
#80	The Roaring River Mystery
#81	The Demon's Den
#82	The Blackwing Puzzle
#83	The Swamp Monster
#84	Revenge of the Desert Phantom
#85	The Skyfire Puzzle
#86	The Mystery of the Silver Star
#87	Program for Destruction
#88	Tricky Business
#89	The Sky Blue Frame
#90	Danger on the Diamond
#91	Shield of Fear
#92	The Shadow Killers
#93	The Serpent's Tooth Mystery
#94	Breakdown in Axeblade
#95	Danger on the Air
#96	Wipeout
#97	Cast of Criminals
#98	Spark of Suspicion
#99	Dungeon of Doom
#100	The Secret of the Island Treasure
#101	The Money Hunt
#102	Terminal Shock
#103	The Million-Dollar Nightmare
#104	Tricks of the Trade
#105	The Smoke Screen Mystery
#106	Attack of the Video Villains
#107	Panic on Gull Island
#108	Fear on Wheels
#109	The Prime-Time Crime
#110	The Secret of Sigma Seven
#111	Three-Ring Terror
#112	The Demolition Mission
#113	Radical Moves
#114	The Case of the Counterfeit Criminals
#115	Sabotage at Sports City
#116	Rock 'n' Roll Renegades
#117	The Baseball Card Conspiracy
#118	Danger in the Fourth Dimension
#119	Touble at Coyote Canyon
#120	The Case of the Cosmic Kidnapping
#121	The Mystery in the Old Mine

Available from MINSTREL Books

121

THE MYSTERY IN
THE OLD MINE

FRANKLIN W. DIXON

PUBLISHED BY POCKET BOOKS

New York   London   Toronto   Sydney   Tokyo   Singapore

This book is a work of fiction. Names, characters, places, and incidents are either the product of the author's imagination or are used fictitiously. Any resemblance to actual events or locales or persons, living or dead, is entirely coincidental.

A MINSTREL PAPERBACK *ORIGINAL*

 A Minstrel Book published by
POCKET BOOKS, a division of Simon & Schuster Inc.
1230 Avenue of the Americas, New York, NY 10020

Copyright © 1993 by Simon & Schuster Inc.
Front cover illustration by Daniel Horne

Produced by Mega-Books of New York, Inc.

ISBN: 0-671-79311-X

First Minstrel Books printing August 1993

10 9 8 7 6 5 4 3 2 1

THE HARDY BOYS MYSTERY STORIES is a trademark of Simon & Schuster Inc.

THE HARDY BOYS, A MINSTREL BOOK, and colophon are registered trademarks of Simon & Schuster Inc.

Printed in the U.S.A.

Contents

1.	Bad News	1
2.	Busted	11
3.	Welcome to Ridge City	21
4.	A Washed-up Clue	30
5.	The Threatening Visitor	41
6.	Code Red!	52
7.	Trapped	59
8.	Into the Mines	68
9.	Cave-in!	81
10.	Buried Alive	90
11.	Running Out of Time	98
12.	Another Break-in	105
13.	Down in the Tunnels	113
14.	A Strange Twist	120
15.	Runaway Train	131
16.	The Great Escape	141

THE MYSTERY IN
THE OLD MINE

1 Bad News

"Wow," Frank Hardy said, running his hands through his dark brown hair. "Someone sure did turn this place upside down."

"You're not kidding," his younger brother, Joe, agreed. "Hey, Garth, watch out for the glass. It's everywhere!"

Frank and Joe Hardy were standing in the middle of their friend Garth Trimmer's bedroom, surrounded by a total mess. All the furniture had been knocked over. Garth's books, CDs, even his weightlifting trophies were strewn across the floor. There was broken glass covering everything.

"When I get my hands on the guy who trashed this place," Garth said between his teeth, "I'm gonna bench press him into the ceiling."

1

Garth clenched his fists, and for a moment Frank saw his mild-mannered friend turn into two hundred and fifty pounds of solid muscle. Tall and good-looking with blond hair, Garth was as gentle as they come. Frank knew he wouldn't really hurt anyone, but he sure looked dangerous when he was angry.

"You said you left your place at ten yesterday morning," Frank said, "and came back from the gym at two."

"So whoever did this had four hours to break in, ransack the place, and get out," Joe concluded. "That's a lot of time."

Garth let out a long sigh. "It sure is. Enough time to completely trash the place, in fact. What's my landlord going to say? I just moved in. This is my first place on my own after college. Now I'm in serious trouble!"

"Chill out, Garth," Joe said, trying to reassure his friend. "We wouldn't let you down."

"You got it," Frank agreed. "That's why you called us in, right?"

The Hardys had met Garth in the gym they worked out at in downtown Bayport. Garth was there all the time, while Frank and Joe only found the time to go when they were between cases. The brothers managed to keep in good shape with other sports. Blond-haired Joe was the more muscular of the two, while Frank was an inch taller at six feet one.

2

Garth knew that the Hardys were experienced detectives, even though Frank was only eighteen and Joe seventeen. When someone broke into his apartment the day before, Garth asked Frank and Joe to help him find out who would want to ransack the place.

"Did the police find any clues?" Frank asked.

Garth shook his head. "If they did, they didn't tell me."

Frank took out a notebook and made a note to call Con Riley, a detective they knew at the Bayport Police Department. "So what's missing, Garth?" he asked.

"That's the thing," Garth said, pacing the room. "Nothing, as far as I can tell."

"I guess it's hard to know," Joe said, pointing to the pile of books, CDs, and laundry on the floor. "Looks like a landfill area."

Garth laughed for the first time since Frank and Joe had arrived. "I guess it's still a mess, huh? I was going to clean up this morning. I even got up super early, but I just couldn't face it. I managed to get the plywood up over the broken window. Then I decided to head for the gym and blow off some of my stress."

"It's a good thing you didn't clean it up," Frank said, removing the plywood. Beneath the wood the window was edged with jagged broken glass. "This way we can see if there are any clues the police might have missed."

3

"Right," Joe agreed.

Together, the Hardys examined the shattered glass and the area underneath it. "We know one thing. Our culprit is probably an amateur," Frank said.

"Why do you say that?" Garth asked from where he sat on the edge of the bed.

"Most of the time pros don't have to break in," Joe pointed out. "They pick the lock and walk in like they own the place."

Frank searched the window frame and the overturned set of bookshelves underneath it for clues. Among the books and broken glass he spotted a number of short, orange hairs.

"Check this out," Frank said to Joe, pointing at the hair.

Joe got down on one knee to look closer. "You don't have a cat or a dog, do you, Garth?" he asked.

Garth shook his head. "Nope. Why do you ask?"

Frank reached into his belt pack and drew out a pair of tweezers and a small plastic bag. He knelt beside Joe and picked up several of the hairs and put them into the bag.

"Because if you don't have a pet, whoever broke into your place sure does," Frank told him. "We'll check out these hairs. My guess is they're from a dog. What do you think, Joe?"

"Looks like it," Joe agreed as he stood up. "They're too long and too thick to be cat hair."

Garth's eyes traveled back and forth from Frank to Joe. Then he smiled wide and said, "I'm sure glad I ran into you guys this morning."

"So are we," Joe said with a laugh. "If you hadn't come along with a new case, Frank was about to get us started on a serious lifting program."

"Maybe afterward," Garth joked. "You know what they say: There's no such thing as being too pumped up."

"Yeah, right," Joe said.

"Too bad we still don't know why this person broke into your apartment," Frank said slowly as his eyes scanned the room.

"Maybe once we pick up some of this stuff, you'll be able to tell what's missing," Joe suggested.

For the next hour Frank and Joe helped Garth clear the mess from the bedroom and vacuum up the broken glass. Garth called a glass repair shop to get the bedroom window replaced. Frank and Joe went into the living room to search for clues while Garth ordered pizzas for an early dinner. Half an hour later Frank had found five more dog hairs but nothing else.

When the front doorbell rang, Garth went to answer it. "Probably the pizza," he said.

Joe entered the living room. "I sure hope so. I'm starving."

When Garth opened the front door, it wasn't the pizza delivery man, but a guy from the glass repair company, standing there in a pair of overalls.

5

"What's wrong?" the repair person asked, seeing their disappointed expressions.

"Uh, nothing," Joe said. "Come on in. We just thought you might be the pizza guy."

"Sorry, dudes. No pizza, just glass. Where's the broken window?"

Garth showed the man into his bedroom, then came back out into the living room to help the Hardys clean up the rest of the mess.

"I still can't tell what the guy took," Garth said in frustration. "My stereo's still here, and so is my TV and VCR. What was he looking for?"

Just then the bell rang a second time. Joe raced for the door. "This has to be the pizza guy," he said. Opening the door with a flourish, he exclaimed, "Yes, we sure did order the two super supreme pizzas with everything on them except anchovies!"

A woman from the local courier company stood in the doorway. "I hate to disappoint you," she said with a smile, "but all I've got is a letter for Garth Trimmer."

Joe stood aside. "That's him," he said weakly, pointing to Garth.

Garth stepped forward and signed for the letter. The delivery woman left, and Garth started opening the envelope.

"Hey, this letter is from Carson, Pennsylvania," he remarked. "That's a city near my hometown, Ridge City. Must be from my sister, Liz." Garth slipped the letter out of the envelope. Frank and Joe stood by as their friend read the note. Suddenly Garth's hands started to shake and his face went white.

"What's wrong?" Joe asked.

Dazed and confused, Garth looked up at the Hardys. "Somebody's sent me a ransom note."

"What?" Frank and Joe exclaimed in unison.

"Look." Garth handed the letter over to Frank and sank down into a nearby chair.

Frank saw the letter was typed on plain white paper. "'Meet me at the covered bridge tonight at midnight. And bring the notebook,'" he read aloud. "'Or else you'll never see your sister, Elizabeth, again.'"

"Whoa," Joe said, taking the letter from Frank. "This is serious stuff."

"No kidding," Garth said in a monotone. He was staring straight ahead, and his face was still incredibly pale.

"Are you okay?" Frank asked, putting a hand on his arm.

"Yeah," Garth assured him. "I'm fine." He shook his head several times, obviously trying to clear his thoughts.

"What's this about a notebook?" Joe asked, scanning the letter and the envelope it came in.

Garth shrugged. "You got me. I don't understand any of this. First somebody breaks into my apartment, now some nutcase has kidnapped my sister."

He sprang up from the chair. "What am I doing?" he cried. "I can't just sit here. My sister could be in real danger. We've got to go help her!"

Frank held his hands up. "Now, hold on a minute," he said. "This letter could be a hoax. You didn't even know your sister was missing, did you?"

"No, I guess I didn't," Garth admitted. He seemed to calm down. "We should find out if she is, right?"

"Exactly," Frank said. "That's the first step. I get the feeling this note has something to do with the fact that your apartment was ransacked yesterday."

Joe nodded in agreement. "You're probably right," he said, holding up the letter. "Whoever broke in here was looking for this notebook, and when he couldn't find it, he sent this note trying to scare you."

Garth looked even more confused. He ran his fingers through his short blond hair and said, "But what's the deal with the notebook? What notebook?"

The doorbell rang again. This time it really was the pizza being delivered, but suddenly none of the boys was very hungry. Joe paid for the pies and set them down on a nearby coffee table.

Frank took a slice of pizza. "Think," he urged Garth. "The letter came from someone in Ridge City, someone who obviously believes you have a notebook that's valuable."

Garth shot up out of his seat and slapped his

forehead with the palm of his hand. "How could I be so stupid? My sister sent me some books the other day."

Garth raced into his bedroom and came back out with two old books. "Neither of these are notebooks, though." He handed them to Frank and Joe. "I'm going to call home. If something's wrong with my sister, I need to know about it. Now."

The Hardys looked at the books Garth had handed them while their friend went into the kitchen to use the phone.

"The title of this one is *Mysterious Mines*," Joe said, leafing through the book. "It looks like a history of coal mining in Pennsylvania. Here's a chapter on Ridge City."

"This book is about mining, too," Frank said.

Joe lowered his voice. "What's going on, Frank?" he asked. "There was no return address on that envelope. I checked. I say we go to Ridge City tonight and meet the guy there, even if we don't have the notebook."

Frank put a hand on his brother's shoulder. "Take it easy, Joe," he said. "We still don't know if this is a real threat or not."

At that moment Garth came into the living room. One look at his face told Frank that something was seriously wrong.

"I just called home," Garth said. "There wasn't any answer at my sister's house, so I called her friend Angela."

"And?" Joe asked expectantly.

"She told me Liz hasn't been around since yesterday," Garth said. "She didn't show up at work today, and the house is empty. Angela had contacted the sheriff just before I called her." He reached for the letter and held it up. "You guys—whoever wrote this note is serious. My sister really has been kidnapped!"

2 Busted

Garth raced to the hall closet and pulled a large duffel bag from the top shelf.

"If we hurry," he said, "we can get to Ridge City by late tonight and start looking for Liz. We'll take shifts driving. It's still before five, and it should only take us about five, maybe six hours to get there. When I get my hands on that guy, whoever he is, who kidnapped my sister, I'm going to—"

"Take it easy, Garth," Joe said. "We'll get this guy." He picked up the note from where Garth had let it drop. "He says to meet him tonight at the covered bridge. Do you know where that is?"

"Sure I do," Garth said, heading for the bedroom. He emerged a few moments later with his arms full of clothes. The window repair man was right behind him.

"Everything's all set," the repairman said. "New glass and everything. I'll send the bill to your landlord." On his way through the living room, the repairman eyed the pizza cartons. "I see you got your pies."

"Help yourself," Frank said.

"Thanks," the repairman said. He grabbed a slice and headed for the door. "Take it easy."

"Sure," Joe said, closing the door behind him. He went to stand by Garth, who was shoving clothes into his duffel bag. "Did your sister's friend have anything else to say?" Joe asked.

Garth shook his head. "Just that Liz was last seen the day before yesterday. Angela said she was about to call me, but she didn't want me to get all worried. There's a chance Liz just took off for a few days."

"Is that like her?" Frank wanted to know.

Garth thought for a moment. "Maybe." He made a face. "I don't know. All I know is right now I'm really worried. I just want to get in my car and drive as fast as we can to Ridge City."

"Let's take our van," Joe suggested as he grabbed another slice. "There's room in the back for one of us to stretch out. We'll need to stop by our place first and pack some clothes."

"Whatever," Garth said, zipping his duffel shut. "So long as it's fast."

* * *

12

By five Frank was heading the van onto the interstate. Garth was next to him, and Joe was sitting in the back. It was exciting to be on a case again, and Joe's mind raced forward to later that night when they'd be meeting the person who sent Garth the note. There was still a lot to set up in the meantime.

"We should call whoever is in charge of the investigation in Ridge City," Joe said. "That person needs to know about the ransom note and that we're coming into town."

"Good idea," Frank agreed. "When we stop for gas, we'll find a pay phone."

Garth eyed the rush-hour traffic. "If this bottleneck keeps up, there's no way we'll be there by midnight."

"Exactly where is Ridge City?" Frank asked, moving into another lane.

"Almost in the very center of Pennsylvania," Garth said. "It's an old mining town. In fact, it's practically an abandoned mining town."

"Why is it abandoned?" Joe asked, leaning forward from the backseat.

"There are underground fires in the tunnels," Garth explained. "It happens in coal-mining regions. A fire starts, the coal is totally flammable, and *whoosh*, you've got a fire burning underground that's completely out of control. Most people have left Ridge City by now, but there are some old diehards who won't go. Like my sister," Garth added softly.

13

"Don't worry, man," Joe reassured him. "We'll find her."

Garth nodded and let out a deep breath. "Sure. That's right. We'll find her."

Frank switched lanes again. Soon they had open road ahead of them, and he got the van up to fifty-five.

"Cruising," Frank said. "I called Con Riley before we left," Frank continued, "and told him about the ransom note. I also mentioned the dog hairs we found, and he said the police found some, too."

"Can they identify the breed?" Joe asked.

"Con said he'd keep me posted," Frank replied. "I told him he could reach us at your sister's house, Garth, and explained what we were doing tonight. He warned us to be careful, like he always does. I told him we knew how to take care of ourselves," Frank said with a chuckle.

"We don't have to worry much," Joe added. "We've got Garth on our side, the champion bodybuilder. He'll watch both our backs."

Around eight o'clock, just as they hit rush-hour traffic north of Philadelphia, Frank decided to stop for gas and coffee. After filling up, he pulled the van over near a pay phone, and the three boys got out.

Joe and Garth listened to the conversation from where they sat on a guardrail. As far as Joe could tell, it was a Sheriff Radford on the other end. Frank explained that he and his brother were detectives. He described the break-in at Garth's and the note Garth had gotten. Frank also told the sheriff about their plan to meet the kidnapper later that night.

"I understand," Frank said. "Yes. I see. No problem. I agree." Finally the older Hardy replaced the phone and turned to Joe and Garth. "Radford's going to stake out the place with some of his men. He doesn't want to be in sight because he thinks that might scare the kidnapper away."

"He's probably right," Joe agreed. "I hope he's close enough to hear us shout for help."

Frank laughed. "I'm sure he will be."

"No news about Liz, I guess?" Garth said, trying not to sound too hopeful.

"Nope," Frank said, shaking his head. "But hey, we'll find her. What's our average these days, Joe?"

"Something like a thousand percent," Joe said, grinning. "Believe it or not."

"I'm not sure I do." Garth returned the grin. "I've seen both you guys lift weights!"

"Hey, hold on," Joe objected, punching Garth on the shoulder.

"I hate to interrupt this," Frank said, "but don't you guys think we need to put together a plan for tonight?"

"Sure thing," Joe said, thinking. "The way I see

15

it, this kidnapper is a complete amateur, especially if he's the same guy who broke into Garth's place. He's probably got Liz hidden away somewhere and plans to set her free as soon as Garth gives him this notebook."

"That sounds right," Frank agreed. "He hasn't made any more contacts with us, as far as we know, and he didn't demand any money."

"There's just one problem," Garth put in. "I don't have the notebook."

"We're going to have to bluff our way through it," Joe said. "You'll meet the guy with a notebook in your hand, any notebook. With any luck he'll want to grab it fast and take off. Even if he doesn't, it won't matter."

"It won't?" Garth asked, confused.

Frank picked up on Joe's idea. "Not a bit. The point is, we'll have our man. We can tail him. The sheriff will be there, too, so with all of us there, we'll catch him."

"And when we do," Joe put in, "he'll have to tell us where your sister is."

"That's brilliant!" Garth cried. A moment later he asked, "But what if we don't catch him?"

Joe glanced at Garth's worried expression and said, "Don't worry, we will."

The Hardys and Garth quickly downed hot dogs and fries inside the snack bar at the rest stop, then stocked up on popcorn and coffee for the road.

Garth spelled Frank at the wheel, and with Joe at

the radio, searching for a station he liked, the three discussed the finer points of their plan.

It was eleven by the time Garth pulled off the interstate and took a dark winding road up into the mountains. Finally they came out of a pass and dropped down a steep incline into Ridge City. The town was darkened, too, with hardly any lights on.

"This place is a little spooky," Joe said as they drove down Main Street. "Like a ghost town."

"I told you," Garth said. He took a right turn off Main Street. "There's still a diner here, and a post office, but otherwise this town is practically dead."

"What's that smell?" Frank asked, sniffing the air. "It's a little like burnt matches—"

"And a lot like rotten eggs," Joe put in.

"That comes from the underground fires," Garth told them. "They give off gas, sulfuric gas. The whole town smells like it. Another reason not to live here. The place stinks."

"Sounds as if you didn't like living here very much," Frank said.

"Hey, it's my hometown," Garth said with a shrug. "I was born and raised here, but I don't have to love it."

The road they were on dead-ended. Garth made a left and pulled up into a driveway. In front of them was a three-story, white Victorian house with a huge front porch in need of a paint job. The lights were out, and the place looked just as abandoned as the town.

17

"This is it. We barely have time to drop off our stuff and go," Garth said, hauling out his gear. "Come on inside."

Once Garth had turned on the lights, the house was actually warm and cheery. There were big comfortable chairs and a couch in the living room, along with a rocking chair. Upstairs, Garth still had his own room. He showed the Hardys the spare room at the end of the hall. There were two twin beds, and Frank and Joe each threw their duffel bags on one.

"My parents died when I was real young," Garth explained once they were back downstairs in the kitchen. "Liz and I kind of raised ourselves—she's nine years older than I am and the only family I've got."

Frank's eyes went to the clock on the wall above the sink. It was already eleven-thirty. "Let's fly," he said. "We've only got half an hour before our kidnapper shows."

"Let's do it," Garth said.

Joe handed Garth a notebook he'd taken out of his duffel bag, and the three friends piled back in the van. Garth drove, taking the road in the direction that led back to town. Before he hit Main Street, however, he made a left turn and climbed into the hills. Soon the road was even darker, and Joe could hear the sound of a river running nearby. After a few miles Garth pulled into a turnoff just before an old covered bridge.

18

"This is the place," he said, shutting off the van.

In the darkness all Joe could hear was the sound of the river rushing by and a few night owls. A half-moon illuminated the area, but the thick trees and undergrowth made it impossible to see if anyone was waiting.

"Let's go," Joe said, pulling open the van's side door.

"Keep low," Frank warned in a whisper.

"Do you see any sign of the sheriff?" Joe asked.

"No," Frank said. "Maybe he's on the other side of the bridge."

Together, the three of them skulked toward the covered bridge. When they got to the entrance, they peered inside, but it was dark and deadly silent. Joe checked his watch again and saw it was still only ten minutes to midnight. "Can't see a thing in there," he said after five minutes of waiting.

"Psst!"

"What was that?" Joe demanded.

"Look!" Garth pointed to the other side of the river, where a lone figure stood near the entrance to the bridge.

"Walk to the middle of the bridge and drop the notebook!" the figure called in a muffled voice. "Then walk back."

"Do it," Joe urged Garth. Joe then turned to Frank. "This is perfect," he whispered. "If we're right and the sheriff's on the other side of the bridge, we've got this guy trapped."

19

"I hope so," Frank said.

Garth walked to the center of the bridge, dropped the notebook, then slowly walked back out. The Hardys heard the figure approach but in the darkness couldn't see anything except a vague outline. The guy was slender and about average height, maybe five feet nine or ten. Joe watched the man stoop down and pick up the book. Then, before Frank or Joe could react, the guy took off at high speed, back in the direction where he'd come from.

Joe waited for the sheriff's men to appear and stop the kidnapper. But no one showed up. The kidnapper ran out the other side of the bridge, then disappeared into the woods by the side of the road.

"Quick!" Joe cried. "He's getting away!"

3 Welcome to
Ridge City

Frank and Joe leapt into action. "Hurry!" Frank yelled. "If we lose this guy, we'll never be able to trace him back to Liz."

Garth realized what was happening and rushed to follow Frank and Joe. Together, the three friends put on the speed and raced across the bridge after the kidnapper, who was fast disappearing deeper into the woods.

Then, behind them, a bright light at the end of the bridge flooded the interior of the bridge. A loud voice called out, "Hold it right there!"

At the opposite end Frank turned around to find himself blinded by a police spotlight.

"Stop running and put your hands in the air!"

In the second it had taken Frank to turn around, Joe and Garth had put on more speed and were following the suspect into the woods.

"What's going on?" Frank demanded, yelling at the spotlight. "Where were you guys?"

"What do you mean, where were we?" the voice cried back. "We were here all the time. Who are you?"

"Well, I'm not the kidnapper, that's for sure," Frank muttered under his breath. "I'm Frank Hardy," he said in a louder voice as he walked back to where the police car was parked. He could see the silhouette of two officers standing in front of the vehicle, although he was blinded by the spotlight and couldn't make out their features. "I'm the one who called you about Liz Trimmer's kidnapping."

"What happened to the other guys?" a young voice asked, shining his flashlight into Frank's eyes.

"Well, I hope they're about to catch our suspect," Frank told the guy, trying to keep calm. "Are you Sheriff Radford?"

The officer shook his head no. "Deputy Gardner. The sheriff is following a lead on the missing person."

"Liz Trimmer," Frank said as he emerged from the covered bridge. He put a hand up to shield his eyes, and the officers turned off the flashlight but kept the spotlight on.

"That's right. So do you want to tell me what

happened here?" Gardner said, taking out a note pad.

"Well, according to Radford, you guys were supposed to help us nail the suspected kidnapper," Frank said curtly. "Only you were supposed to be at the other end of the bridge."

"We were right where we were supposed to be," another officer retorted. Her badge read Jervis. "And when we saw you three arrive and skulk around, we thought you were the kidnappers." At Frank's groan she added defensively, "Well, you did look very suspicious."

At that moment Joe and Garth walked out of the covered bridge. From Joe's crestfallen face, Frank could tell they'd lost the suspect.

"Who are these guys?" Gardner wanted to know.

"That's my brother, Joe, and our friend Garth," Frank told him. "Garth's the one whose sister has been kidnapped."

Gardner and Jervis exchanged a look. "Looks like we lost our man," Gardner said. "Any sign of him in the woods, boys?"

Joe rolled his eyes. "If there were, don't you think we'd have him for you?" he said.

Gardner looked Frank and Joe up and down as if he didn't like their attitudes. Frank decided to cool down. There was nothing they could do now about losing the trail.

Frank let out a long sigh. "Look, we blew this

one. Would you mind getting in touch with Sheriff Radford on your radio to find out what's happening with his lead? I'm sure our friend Garth would appreciate it."

Gardner made a face but leaned into the squad car and reached for his radio. Within a few moments he was talking to Radford. Frank listened in to the conversation. He quickly figured out, between the squawking and the static, that Radford's lead had turned into a dead end.

"Sheriff's hanging it up for the night," Gardner said, replacing the radio. "Seems like that's the thing to do."

Frank kicked at a rock beside his feet. "I guess so," he said, shaking his head. "Come on, Joe, Garth. Let's head out."

"You boys be careful, now," Jervis warned them as they walked away. "There's a kidnapper on the loose."

"Oh, really?" Garth mumbled to Frank. "That's funny—I wouldn't have known that if she hadn't told me."

"What a bust," Joe said once they were back in the van. "So much for Ridge City's finest."

Frank started up the van and headed down the hill, back to Garth's house.

"You see?" Garth said. "Didn't I tell you this town stinks?"

* * *

Early the next morning Frank drove the van down Main Street, heading in the direction of the Ridge City Restaurant. The three friends were going to grab some breakfast and then head into Carson. Frank wanted to find out if the company that delivered the ransom note to Garth could give them a lead on who might have sent it.

"Gosh," Joe said, "almost every store on this street is boarded up."

Garth nodded. "Since the mine fires are getting so close to town, most people have left. My sister said the government's trying to buy the last few diehards out, offering them compensation for having to leave. She says it isn't enough money, and she's fighting for more. Take a left here," Garth instructed.

Frank pulled the van into the gravel parking lot in front of the Ridge City Restaurant. "This is the finest dining in town," Garth remarked. "Actually, it's the only dining in town."

"And we're the only customers," Joe said as he followed Frank and Trimmer into the diner.

"Not quite," said a police officer who was leaving as they were going in. "Sheriff Ed Radford," the man went on. "You must be the Hardys."

"We sure are," Frank said, reaching out to shake the man's hand. Radford was of medium height and looked as if he'd been stocky when he was younger, though he was definitely inching closer to being overweight. "I'm Frank, and this is my brother, Joe. I guess you remember Garth."

"Sure do," Radford said. He jokingly punched Garth in the arm. "You sure have grown, son. I'd be afraid to arm wrestle you now."

Garth smiled and said, "You'd better be."

The sheriff offered to come back inside with Garth and the Hardys while they ate breakfast. "We can go over this case. Terrible thing about your sister, Garth. But don't worry, we're going to find her."

After they were all seated in a booth with a view of Main Street, a waitress came over to take their order. When she saw Garth, her face lit up.

"Garth Trimmer!" the waitress cried. "You son of a gun. Look at you." She leaned over to give him a big hug and a kiss.

"This is Angela Golding," Garth explained, blushing. "She's my sister's friend, the one I called yesterday."

Angela tossed back her dark hair and smiled. "Nice to meet you." Her pretty brown eyes moved from Garth to Frank to Joe, but then the smile faded. "Is there any news about Liz?" she asked, concerned.

"Nothing right now, I'm afraid," the sheriff said. "We had a few leads last night, but nothing bit."

"Where do we go from here?" Joe wanted to know.

26

"First, you order some hot breakfast," the sheriff joked.

Angela held up her pad and waited for their order. When they were done, she brought the sheriff his coffee and juice for Frank, Joe, and Garth.

Finally the sheriff leaned across the table. "We're stuck, boys," he confessed. He shook his head sadly. "Garth, I'm sorry to tell you, but we're at a total dead end. Whatever you kids can do to help, I'm going to welcome it."

"We got an anonymous tip called in last night," Radford explained. "Took us out to the old high school. I went with a few officers to investigate, but we didn't find a thing. I guess my men blew it with you guys and your meeting."

Frank shot Joe a look that warned him to keep a cool head. "When our suspect finds out we didn't pass him the notebook he was looking for, he'll be back in touch," Frank said. "I'm sure of it."

Angela returned with their orders. Garth took his plate of eggs from her. "Let me know if you need anything else," she said.

"You kids didn't have this notebook, then?" the sheriff asked. He took a sip of his coffee and looked at Garth.

"We don't even know what it is," Garth said, taking a bite of toast.

"But you think the guy who broke into your

apartment was looking for it?" the sheriff prodded.

"That's what Frank told me."

"Maybe," Frank said. "It's still confusing. Did the guy break into Garth's house looking for the notebook? When he didn't find it, did he decide to kidnap Liz and hold her for ransom?"

The sheriff raised his eyebrows. "The timing's right. Liz was last seen the day before yesterday, in the evening. I was out of town, but my deputy did some investigating, asked around. She went to a city council meeting that night, but she didn't show up for work the next morning."

"The day before yesterday," Garth said slowly. "That's the same day my place was broken into. Maybe the guy tried to find the notebook and realized he couldn't. Then he drove back to Ridge City and kidnapped Liz."

"Could be," Frank said. "There's still something that doesn't seem right about this, though."

"What's that?" Joe asked.

Before Frank could answer, the door to the diner burst open, and a thin young man came rushing inside.

"That's David Handler," Garth said, half rising out of his seat. "He's my sister's boyfriend."

"He sure looks upset," Joe remarked.

Handler's eyes had a wild look to them. His sandy brown hair was a mess, and his clothes were soaking wet.

"Angela!" he cried, spotting the waitress. He

28

looked around the diner and saw the sheriff, too. "Sheriff Radford! Both of you, come quick. You've got to help."

"Whoa," the sheriff said, standing up. "Calm down, son. What's going on?"

"It's Liz! I found her car. And I think . . ." Handler dropped his face into his hands. "I think . . ." he tried again, looking up in desperation. "I think she's drowned!"

4 A Washed-up Clue

Finally Handler calmed down enough to speak. "I was driving past Sassafras Run," he told them, "when I saw a car in the river. I recognized it right away. It's Liz's car, there's no doubt about it."

Angela put her hand to her face and cried, "Oh, no!"

Joe kept his eyes on Garth. Their friend looked pale, but he was holding up pretty well. In fact, Garth was the first one to get up. "Let's go," he called, tossing some money on the counter to pay for his breakfast.

Within minutes Frank was pulling the van onto a shoulder beside the spot where Handler had seen Liz's car. Handler had driven ahead of them, and the sheriff followed behind.

30

Frank parked on the shoulder and turned off the engine. Joe climbed out and scrambled down the rugged bank toward the creek.

"Joe!" Frank called out. "Over there!"

Joe looked in the direction his brother was pointing. A small, white foreign car was upside down at the bottom of the creek. Joe could see that the driver's side door was open and falling off its hinges.

"Can you see anyone inside?" Frank asked as he reached the bank next to Joe.

"I don't see anyone," he replied as he squatted on the bank and looked at the car. "The water's too swift to jump in."

The sheriff came to stand beside them on the riverbank.

Handler was right behind. "Maybe Liz was driving in it and got washed off the road." He sighed deeply.

Joe exchanged a look with Frank. Obviously David Handler didn't want to believe Liz had been kidnapped. "You think she had an accident?" he asked Handler.

The sheriff spoke up before Handler could answer Joe's question. "David and I have been through this. He's convinced Liz wasn't kidnapped."

"You still don't have any proof she was kidnapped," Handler asserted.

Garth stepped up and put a reassuring hand on David's shoulder. "We do have proof, David," he

31

said softly. As soon as Garth told David about the ransom note, Handler's face fell.

"Well, if she were kidnapped, at least she'd be alive," David said. "On the other hand, it could be a hoax."

Joe's blue eyes swept the river. "Look," he said, "maybe we'll have a better idea of what happened here once the car is searched."

"Good idea, Joe," the sheriff agreed. "I'm going to call headquarters. We'll need a tow truck with a winch if we're going to get that car out of there." With that, the sheriff started walking back up the riverbank in the direction of his squad car.

Within fifteen minutes a tow truck appeared, along with several other squad cars. Among them, Joe spotted Gardner, the deputy they'd met the night before, and his partner, Jervis. The two of them stood next to the sheriff, conferring about the best way to rescue the car.

"What's the deal with Handler?" Frank wondered aloud, out of earshot of either Garth or David. "He seems pretty convinced Liz wasn't kidnapped."

Joe shrugged. "You got me," he said. "I say we question him after we're done here."

Meanwhile, the tow truck driver had attached a cable to the car and was winching the car out of the creek. Soon the car landed on the riverbank with a terrible groan of metal. The driver coiled the cable further and the car was dragged over the bank to the side of the road.

Joe and Frank rushed to the car and were examining it in an instant. "No signs of a collision," Joe said aloud to his brother. "The whole thing's pretty battered, but none of these dents look as if they were made by another car."

The sheriff came over, along with his deputy and Officer Jervis. The officers searched the inside of the car and found Liz's soggy registration and insurance cards. There were no other personal belongings in the car.

"Weird," Joe said to Frank.

"What is?" Garth asked.

Joe thought for a moment. "Either the kidnapper ran her car into the river because he wanted to make it look as if she had an accident—"

"Or she really did have an accident," David Handler finished.

The sheriff instructed the tow truck driver to take the car back to the police station, then Radford hopped back in his squad car and took off after the tow truck.

"Why are you so sure Liz had an accident?" Garth asked Handler in a low voice. "I told you about the note I got, and how we met the kidnapper last night."

Handler's eyes traveled back and forth from Frank to Joe to Garth. He dragged a hand through his already messy hair and thought for a moment.

33

"Is there something you want to tell us?" Joe asked.

Handler paused, then said, "No, no, there isn't. Look, I'm late for an appointment. I've really got to go." He took off at a clip and got into his car, leaving the Hardys and Garth alone.

"Was David Handler always this strange a guy?" Joe asked Garth.

Garth crossed his arms over his chest, thinking. "I'm not sure. He and my sister always had this on-again, off-again relationship, though. By the time I left for college four years ago, it was mostly off, I think. Angela would know better than I would what kind of guy he is."

"Do you think he'd do anything to harm your sister?" Joe asked.

Garth looked shocked. "No way. I mean, I really doubt it," he said, shaking his head vigorously.

"Wait a minute, Joe," Frank put in. "As far as we know, Handler's concerned about Liz. Why suspect him?"

Joe picked up a rock and tossed it into the river. "You saw him just now," he said. "He was covering something up, I know it."

Frank let out a long sigh.

"I know what you're thinking," Joe said. "I always leap to conclusions. I'm not looking at the facts clearly. I'm telling you, Frank, the guy is guilty of something. I just need to figure out what."

"Well, right now I think our best bet is to head

back to Garth's place," Frank said, "and see what, if anything, your sister left behind—before her mysterious disappearance."

"Which David Handler insists was an accident," Joe said with a snort.

Frank ignored his brother and said, "We can call the courier service in Carson. With any luck they can help us over the phone."

Ten minutes later the Hardys and Garth were back at the Trimmer house, searching it from top to bottom for some kind of clue.

"What are we looking for?" Garth asked Joe as they looked through Liz's downstairs den.

Joe glanced up from the desk where he was searching the drawers. "Anything," he said. "A note, a diary, an address book. Something that might tell us what Liz was doing the days before she disappeared."

"You think there's a connection between what she was doing and the fact that she disappeared?" Garth asked.

"There's always a chance," Joe said. He kept up his search of the desk drawers.

Frank came into the den, scratching his head. "I called the courier service in Carson. They said the letter was dropped off right as they were closing. Whoever brought it left cash to pay for the delivery. There's no record of who it was."

"So that's a dead end," Joe said in frustration.

"Meanwhile," Frank went on, "all Liz's clothes

35

are here, and there's no sign of a forced entry anywhere in the house. We need to find out more about when and where Liz disappeared."

"Right," Joe said. "You know, it's strange, but all of these drawers are empty. There are no papers here, no bills, nothing. Hold on—"

Frowning, he pulled out a square piece of paper buried deep inside the top desk drawer. It had Garth's name printed on the outside. Joe handed it to their friend.

Garth unfolded the paper and gave the Hardys a curious look. "It's a flier announcing an upcoming city council meeting. But why is my name written on the outside of the paper?"

"Maybe Liz left it for you," Joe suggested.

Frank took the paper from Garth. "That means Liz guessed that Garth would come home and find this paper."

"This is totally strange," Garth said. "Do you think she knew she was in danger and left this note for me in case something happened to her?"

Joe looked at the announcement over Frank's shoulder. "Hey, that meeting's this afternoon! At two o'clock."

"It's one now," Frank said. "We'd better hurry if we want to be there."

"Just let me finish searching her desk," Joe said. "Maybe there's something else here that I missed."

Joe ran his hands around the inside of each drawer and along the underside of the desk. Suddenly his hands felt another piece of paper, this one stuck with tape to the bottom of the center drawer. He peeled it off and saw it was an envelope. "Garth!" he exclaimed when he saw that Garth's name was written on it. Joe handed the envelope to Garth, who ripped it open eagerly and unfolded the note inside.

"It's a map of the mine tunnels," Garth said, obviously confused. "That's all. No note, nothing else. Just a map, signed 'Love, Liz.'" Garth looked over the map carefully, then handed it and the envelope to Joe, who looked at them both several times.

"Guess what?" Joe asked, holding up the map and the envelope. He looked at the flier that was on top of the desk.

"What?" Frank asked.

"This map and the flier were left by two different people," Joe said excitedly.

"They were?" Garth demanded.

"Sure enough." Joe pointed out the handwriting on the map and the envelope it came in. "This script isn't the same as the handwriting on the outside of the flier."

Frank looked carefully. "You're right," he said. "Which handwriting belongs to Liz?"

Garth studied the flier and the envelope for a moment. "That's Liz's handwriting on the map envelope," he said finally. "What do you think it means?"

"Liz wanted you to have the map, but somebody else left you this flier," Frank concluded, looking at his watch. "Meanwhile, we'd better head downtown if we want to make that meeting."

In the van on the way to the city council meeting, Joe, Frank, and Garth tried to make sense of the latest leads in the case.

"I'm sure Liz must have known she was in danger," Joe said as he made a turn onto Main Street. "She couldn't be down in the mines, could she? Why else would she have left a map for Garth? You weren't planning to come home in the near future, were you?"

"Not on your life!" Garth joked. He got serious a second later. "It scares me to think my sister thought she was in danger. And then something bad did happen to her. It's creepy. I can't believe she'd go down to those mine tunnels—they're dangerous, and the air is bad. Anyway, I doubt there's a way to get down there. The entrances should all be sealed up."

Frank tried to reassure their friend. "We'll talk to the sheriff and see what he knows about the mines. In the meantime, we'll do all the legwork that we can to help us understand why she disappeared and who might have kidnapped her. Unless our kidnapper sends us another note, there's nothing more to do."

"Right," said Garth softly. "It's just that I get more worried as time goes by."

"Is this the place?" Joe said, driving slowly past a two-story building with a flagpole in front. Bronze letters spelled out the words City Hall on the building's brick face.

"Sure is," Garth said. "Smallest city hall this side of Philadelphia. Welcome to Ridge City, smallest everything this side of Philadelphia!"

Joe parked the van, and Garth and the Hardys walked inside the building. On their right as they entered there was a small auditorium with open doors. Joe led the way into the room, and the three friends found seats in one of the back rows.

Within a few minutes the room had filled with people, and a dark-haired woman in a red suit was calling the meeting to order. She had a sign in front of her that read Mayor Lucy Stephenson. Joe spotted David Handler among the crowd, sitting next to Angela Golding.

"We have a plan here to approve a government proposal to buy out those residents of Ridge City who still remain," the mayor said, adjusting the microphone in front of her. "The government is offering compensation to the townspeople for the loss of homes and property and for moving expenses. We're here to listen to public comment. Three days from now the council will vote on this proposal."

For several minutes the Hardys listened to the residents come forward to express their views. Joe was starting to get bored, and he was wondering who on earth had left the flier for Garth to find. Then Angela Golding approached the microphone that had been set up for the public.

"Mayor Stephenson," she began in a shaky voice, "I know Liz Trimmer would have spoken here today . . . if she could." Angela reached for a tissue, blew her nose, and went on. "But she can't, so I will—"

"What's going on here?" Frank leaned over to whisper in Joe's ear. "What was Liz involved in?"

"Don't know," Joe whispered back. "But I think we're about to find out."

"Liz Trimmer fought long and hard to save this town," Angela said, reading from some notes. "I know she'd be against this proposal. I know she'd say we weren't getting enough from the government. I know she'd talk about how Yankee Stalwart—"

"Ms. Golding," Mayor Stephenson interrupted, "that will be enough."

"I have a right to speak!" Angela insisted.

"And I have a right to tell you this!" the mayor shouted, leaning into her microphone. "Liz Trimmer isn't here, and I'm glad. I've had just about enough of her troublemaking! I for one am in favor of this proposal."

The mayor scanned the crowd with her flashing green eyes. "In fact," she said, her face growing red as she became more enraged, "if Liz Trimmer never shows up again, it won't be too soon for me!"

5 The Threatening Visitor

Frank moved to the edge of his seat and listened carefully as Mayor Stephenson went on.

"That woman would have single-handedly defeated a critical economic package for this community," the mayor insisted.

"But, Mayor—" Angela tried to speak.

"But nothing."

Around them the crowd began to buzz. "The mayor's right!" a man beside Frank shouted.

"She sure is," a woman on the other side of the room put in.

"Ridge City needs this plan!" someone else shouted.

"This place is turning into a mob scene," Frank

41

said to Garth. "Did you have any idea of what your sister was involved with?"

Garth's eyes went wide. "No, I didn't. From what the mayor just said, though, I'm starting to think a lot of people in this room are pretty happy that my sister's disappeared."

"Including the mayor," Joe put in.

Throughout this whole scene Frank noticed that David Handler was being strangely silent. At one point Angela even turned to him and held out her hands, as if she was begging him to step in and help her out. Handler just shook his head and buried himself in his seat.

"Order! Order!" the mayor shouted.

The five council members spoke among themselves, gesturing to the audience and the mayor.

Finally the council member nearest Lucy Stephenson leaned into the microphone and said, "Until order is restored, I suggest we call this meeting to a recess, Mayor."

Another council member spoke up. "I second Councilman Brennan's motion."

"So ordered!" The mayor shoved her microphone away and stood up. Several members of the audience tried to speak to her, but Mayor Stephenson was out the door of the auditorium before anyone could stop her.

"What was all that about?" Joe muttered to Frank.

Frank got up from his seat, trying to keep his eyes

on Angela Golding and David Handler. From where he stood, it looked as if Angela and David were exchanging words. Angela raised her voice several times, but Frank was too far away to hear what she was saying.

"This just blows my mind," Garth said, shaking his head sadly. He sat slumped in his seat while around them, residents of Ridge City moved toward the exit in clusters. "I guess Liz stirred up some real trouble this time." Garth heaved himself out of his chair. "What are we going to do now?" he asked Frank and Joe.

Joe ran his hands through his hair. "Good question. We've gone from having no suspects to having a whole room full of them. Seems that almost everyone here was against Liz."

Angela spotted them at the back of the auditorium and came rushing over. David Handler was right behind her. He didn't stop to say hello but went right on out the door.

"I can't believe him!" Angela exclaimed, her face red with anger. "For someone who claims to love Liz, he sure doesn't stick up for her."

"What happened just now?" Frank asked.

Angela tapped her foot impatiently. "I wanted David to get up and say something in Liz's defense, but he said it was hopeless. Everyone's against her, he said, and everyone's in favor of the plan. He thinks it wasn't worth fighting for. Brother! So why did he bother coming, then? Explain that."

Frank realized that there was a lot Angela knew, and a lot they could learn from her, about what had been going on in Ridge City politics.

"Listen," Frank said, watching the room empty. "Are you free for lunch? I know I'm starving, and I thought maybe we could ask you a few questions about Liz."

Angela brightened considerably. She said, "Sure. I know just the place!"

Ten minutes later the Hardys, Garth, and Angela were sitting in a red vinyl-covered booth at the Ridge City Restaurant. "So what did you want to know?" Angela asked, taking a sip of her iced tea.

Frank rubbed his chin thoughtfully. "Do you think Liz's disappearance is connected to what just went on in that meeting?"

Angela swallowed hard and looked afraid for an instant. "Yes, yes, I do," she said softly.

The waitress came to the table with their orders. While she was handing over the plates, Frank was quiet. Once she left, Joe asked Angela, "What makes you so sure?"

"Did Liz think she was in danger?" Garth asked before Angela could answer Joe's question.

"She sure did," Angela said breathlessly, then lowered her voice. "She was getting threats."

Frank felt his excitement rising. "Do you know who they were from?"

Angela shook her head and took a bite of her sandwich. "No. She wasn't sure. It was phone calls at night mostly." Angela narrowed her eyes. "People in this town don't appreciate that Liz was fighting for them. Between Yankee Stalwart and the mine fires, the government owes us."

"What's Yankee Stalwart?" Joe wanted to know.

"That's the nuclear power plant outside of town," Garth informed him, popping a french fry into his mouth. "They used to hire the whole town, but now they're down to a skeleton crew. They don't have to, but they decided that it was too dangerous to operate a nuclear power plant so near the mine fires."

"Liz works for them," Angela explained. "She's in personnel. David Handler used to work there, too. Liz said the government should pay a generous severance to Ridge City employees who lost their jobs, but the government wasn't going to, especially since the plant is closing voluntarily. They said all they could cover was the damage from the mine fires. It's considered relief for a natural disaster. You want a disaster? Look at what's happening in this town. The unemployment rate is the real disaster."

Frank took a sip of his cola and thought about what Angela was saying. "The people here seem to be willing to accept the government's offer."

Angela sighed. "Liz was sure there was a way to get more of a settlement. She was going to fight the mayor's proposal, no matter what. She was determined," Angela said proudly. "But in three days the mayor's going to put the proposal to a vote in city council, and that'll be that. If Liz doesn't turn up to fight it, I'd bet you anything it will pass."

"Does the mayor have much to gain here?" Joe wanted to know.

"She sure does," Angela said, her voice rising with emotion. "The proposal pays her a salary for three whole years! That's how long the government thinks it will take to clear out Ridge City for good."

"Then the town will really be dead," Garth said. His voice sounded almost sad.

"Hey," Frank pointed out, "I thought you said this town stinks."

They all laughed then, and Garth said, "Well, it does. But I never wanted it to shut down completely. It's my hometown! If Ridge City dies, where'll I tell people I grew up? An abandoned town outside of Pittsburgh?"

Angela smiled at Garth and elbowed him playfully. "Shucks. Now, that really would stink!"

The four quickly finished off their lunch, since Angela's shift was scheduled to start at three. After she got up to punch in, Joe rested his elbows on the table and said, "So where do we go from here?"

Frank downed the rest of his soda, then said, "I think we need to talk to Mayor Stephenson. Then I say we head out to Yankee Stalwart and talk to whoever is in charge."

"That would be Adam Brill," Garth told them. "I've heard my sister mention him before."

Joe reached for the check, but Angela called out

46

from behind the counter, "Hey, it's on me. When we find Liz, you can buy dinner!"

"Thanks," Frank said, leaving a tip. "I'm going to call the mayor and see if she has some time to see us."

Frank went to the pay phone by the door. As he was making the call, David Handler entered the diner. Frank quickly found out from the mayor's secretary that Lucy Stephenson didn't have any time to see them until the next day. Frank made an appointment for the afternoon.

While Frank was on the phone, he spotted Joe talking to Handler. The two of them exchanged a few words, and then Joe joined Garth out in the parking lot. As soon as Frank got off the phone, he went outside.

"What was all that about with Handler?" Frank asked his brother.

Joe smiled and shrugged. "Nothing really. I just asked him if he would be around later for us to stop by. I said I wanted to ask him a few questions. Boy, did he jump."

"David didn't seem as if he wanted to talk to us before," Garth mentioned.

"And I don't really want to talk to him," Joe said, smiling wide now. "I just wanted to find out when he'd be home. He said he'd be in karate class until six-thirty. That means it's safe until then for us to search his place."

Frank rolled his eyes. "Give it up, okay, Joe? We

47

are not going out to search David Handler's place. We don't have any proof that he's involved."

Joe grunted with frustration. "How else are we going to get proof?" he muttered. "Look, I just want to investigate. Hey, we're detectives, right? And detectives investigate, right? So what's wrong?"

Frank opened the driver's side door and hopped into the van. Joe and Garth got in from the other side.

"Nothing." Frank paused, thinking it over. "Okay," he said finally. "After Yankee Stalwart, we can stop by Handler's place. Are you happy now?"

Joe grinned from ear to ear. "Now, that's the Frank Hardy I know."

As the three friends headed out to Yankee Stalwart, Frank said, "If Liz was stirring up trouble at Yankee Stalwart, chances are Adam Brill will have something to say about it."

On their way out of town they passed the police station. "I'm going to stop in," Frank told Joe. "We can find out if there have been any leads in the case on this end."

Things were quiet at the Ridge City station. Joe asked if there were any breaks in the case. The dispatcher told them that the sheriff was out on another lead, but that she hadn't heard a word yet about whether or not it paid off.

"For a town where someone's apparently been

48

kidnapped, things sure are calm," Joe said as they left the parking lot.

Garth bit on the end of his fingernail. "I feel as if I should be at home, just in case the kidnapper tries to contact me again. He must know by now that we didn't give him the book he was looking for."

"If you think about it," Frank said, pulling back onto the highway, "hardly anything about this case makes sense. Your place is broken into, but you can't tell what's missing. You get a ransom note for a notebook you don't have. Liz may or may not have been kidnapped. Her old boyfriend is convinced she had an accident but won't tell us why. The whole town is full of people who might have wanted Liz out of the way."

"Don't forget the flier someone left Garth," Joe put in.

"And the map Liz taped to the underside of her desk," Garth reminded Frank.

"I'd like to make another list," Frank said. "Of the things we do know—but I have a feeling that side of the page would be empty!"

Just then they passed a sign reading Yankee Stalwart: 1 Mile. Within a few minutes Frank was driving into the plant's entrance.

"I can't believe they put a nuclear power plant in a town with underground fires," Frank said, pulling into a parking space.

"The fires started after the plant was built,"

Garth told them. "But it's definitely a big problem, especially because some of the old mine shafts run right up to the power plant. There are underground walls that protect the plant, but I guess the Yankee management decided that wasn't enough."

The three friends walked toward the entrance of the sprawling glass and steel factory. The buildings were high-tech, and there were huge antennas and satellite dishes on all the rooftops. The complex was empty, almost spooky, with no sign of human life.

When Frank, Joe, and Garth entered the Yankee Stalwart offices, the place was deathly quiet. A lone receptionist answered the phones, but they weren't exactly ringing off the hook. One other person was sitting in the reception area.

"We're here to see Adam Brill," Frank informed the receptionist. "We don't have an appointment, but do you think he could find a few minutes for us?"

"And what is this in reference to?" the red-haired receptionist asked.

"It's about Liz Trimmer," Joe told her.

The receptionist raised her eyebrows, then asked them to have a seat. "I'll page Mr. Brill. Unfortunately, you're not the only people asking to see him. You might have to wait."

Frank thanked the woman, and the three friends took a seat opposite the man, who was also waiting for Brill. He was in his mid-thirties and had black hair shot through with gray. The man was wearing jeans and a button-down shirt and had a beat-up briefcase on the floor next to him.

"Excuse me," the man said, leaning close. "Did I hear you mention the name Liz Trimmer?"

Frank shot Joe a curious look. "Yes, yes, you did," he said.

The man bent even closer, and whispered, "Did you know she's disappeared?" he asked, narrowing his eyes.

"We did," Garth said. "She's my sister."

"Oh." The man sat back in his chair with a shocked look on his face. "Hey, I'm really sorry. Listen, the name's Mauer, Fred Mauer. I'm a reporter for the *Pittsburgh Gazette*—"

Just then a door at the end of the reception area burst open and a slender, distinguished-looking man in a dark suit came through. He stood by the reception desk and said in a deep voice, "I'm Adam Brill."

"Brill!" Mauer cried out.

Suddenly the reporter was on his feet, rushing toward the factory's president.

"I made a promise to Liz Trimmer!" Mauer shouted. "If something ever happened to her, I was going to come out here and nail you!"

And before anyone could stop him, Fred Mauer had wrapped his hands around Adam Brill's throat and started to strangle him!

51

6 Code Red!

"Mauer!" Joe called out, rushing to pull the man off Brill.

The reporter's hands were clenched around Adam Brill's neck, and the plant president's face was turning bright red.

"Hetty!" Brill gagged. "Call the police. Now!"

The receptionist snapped out of her shocked trance and had the phone off the hook in a second. Meanwhile, at the mention of the word *police*, Mauer let his hands drop from Brill's neck.

The reporter took a few steps back, and with a hard edge in his voice, he said, "You haven't seen the last of me, Brill. I'm going to get you—and Yankee Stalwart. For Liz Trimmer and everyone else out there who believes in the environment!"

With that, Mauer pushed past Joe, Frank, and

Garth. He grabbed his briefcase and disappeared through the plant's front doors, letting them slam behind him.

Joe let out a low whistle. "Wow," he said. "Talk about chips on your shoulder. Are you okay?" he asked Brill, looking the man over carefully.

Adam Brill loosened his tie with one hand and reached for the handkerchief in his breast pocket with the other.

"I'm fine, boys," Brill said, "just fine. Sorry about that altercation. Apparently Mr. Mauer doesn't think very highly of me." He sighed. "If only he'd cool down, he'd realize that we're both on the same side. I believe in the environment, too. That's why I'm shutting Yankee Stalwart down. The risk of operating a plant so close to the mine fires is too high."

Brill turned to the receptionist. "Cancel that call to the police, please. I doubt we'll be seeing much more of Mr. Mauer."

Brill turned to face Garth and the Hardys. "What can I do for you guys?"

Frank cleared his throat and said, "Actually, we're here about Liz Trimmer, too."

"That's what Hetty told me." Brill eyed all three of them evenly. "You're not reporters, are you?" he joked. "Because after what just happened, I'd have to say no comment!"

Joe laughed and said, "No. We're trying to locate Liz Trimmer."

53

"Oh, really?" Brill said.

"Frank and Joe Hardy," Garth said, introducing them. "I'm Garth Trimmer. Liz is my sister."

Brill shook all their hands, then told Garth, "I'm sorry to hear about Liz. Anything I can do to help, let me know. Liz was a valuable employee, even if some people on the management side didn't always agree with her."

"I think maybe you *can* help us," Joe said. "We've learned that Liz Trimmer was fighting a government proposal to give money to residents of Ridge City. She thinks the government should also provide money for people who lost their jobs at Yankee Stalwart. What's your opinion about all this?" he asked.

Brill cleared his throat and put the handkerchief back in his pocket. "Perhaps we should discuss this in my office," he said. With that, he ushered Frank, Joe, and Garth through a door that led back into the plant itself.

They walked down a glass-enclosed hallway that gave them a view of the plant operations. Most of the rooms they passed were empty, but here and there Joe saw a few workers in white overalls, wearing masks and gloves.

Brill opened a door in front of them with his security key. "I'd show you more of the plant, but we're in the process of cleaning up the entire premises. An official government inspection team is

54

coming through here next week. They want to be sure we've closed down operations according to all the rules and regulations."

They passed through a part of the plant that consisted of two big rooms on either side of a glassed-in walkway. The rooms were full of gleaming metal machinery. Gigantic tubes ran from floor to ceiling. There were dials and lights on the tubes, and all along the outside walls were control panels. A few workers sat at these consoles, monitoring the controls. The workers wore white coveralls, masks, and gloves.

At the end of the hall Brill turned right, into a corridor lined with offices. Along the way he stopped at a secretary's desk to pick up his messages.

"Have a seat, boys," Brill said, opening his office door and gesturing for them to step inside. "Can I get you anything? Soda?"

"No, thanks," Joe said. He sat down in a plush leather chair facing Brill's desk. Frank took the chair to Joe's left, and Garth sat down on a sofa to the right.

"Did you know the sheriff was investigating the possibility that Liz Trimmer was kidnapped?" Frank asked.

Brill rested his arms on his desk and let out a long sigh. "I did hear that. At first, I guess he thought she had simply disappeared."

"But then I got a ransom note," Garth said.

Joe decided to test a theory. "Mr. Brill, do you know Liz's boyfriend, David Handler?"

Brill raised his eyebrows. "Everyone in town knows David Handler. He even worked here for a while. Some people think David's a kook, but I've always found him to be likable."

Joe rubbed his chin thoughtfully, then glanced at Frank. "We think there are a lot of people in this town who would like to see Liz out of the way. Could Handler be one of them?" he asked.

Brill managed a grim smile. "I'm afraid you're right about people wanting Liz out of the way. Sorry to say that, Garth. The town's in favor of the government proposal to buy out the last remaining homeowners and resettle them elsewhere. There's money in that plan to clear this place out and let nature take over again."

"What about the jobs lost here at Yankee Stalwart?" Frank asked. "Liz was fighting to get money for those unemployed people, wasn't she?"

"That's a separate issue," Brill said, shaking his head. "It depends on what the federal unemployment compensation policy is in the case of natural disasters."

At that moment there was a knock on the door. A woman in her late thirties popped her head in the door. "Adam? When you get a chance?"

"Sure thing. Hey, Jackie, come on in. I want you to meet these guys." Brill stood up and made the

56

introductions. "Jackie George, this is Garth Trimmer and his friends Frank and Joe Hardy. Liz Trimmer is Garth's older sister."

Jackie shook their hands and gave them all a bright smile. "Has she been found?" she asked excitedly.

Garth shook his head sadly. "Not yet," he said.

"Jackie is our government liaison working on closing down Yankee Stalwart. She also drafted the proposal for compensation for the mine fires," Brill explained. "If you have any questions about the proposal, Jackie's the one to ask. You even talked to Liz a bit, didn't you, Jackie?"

Jackie nodded her head, then looked down to the waistband of her jeans, where a beeper was flashing silently. "Sorry, Adam, that's a call I have to take. Can I see you later this afternoon? I have some figures to go over with you before the meeting tomorrow."

"Sure," Brill agreed. After Jackie left the room, Brill turned to Joe. "We're having a meeting tomorrow about the proposal. I'm on the executive committee along with a couple of the Yankee Stalwart people, so the meeting's here. Why don't you boys come? You'll get the inside track on all the figures, plus you'll be able to ask some questions. I know Mayor Stephenson's coming."

Brill's voice was suddenly drowned out by a piercing whine.

57

Joe looked at Frank. "The emergency alarm!" Frank shouted.

Brill jumped up from his desk and raced to the door. As soon as he opened it, Joe could see lights flashing up and down the hall. Meanwhile, the siren continued to blare.

Over the loud wail a voice shouted on the plant intercom, "Code Red! Attention! This is a Code Red emergency! This is not a drill. Repeat. This is *not* a drill!"

7 Trapped

Frank sprang to his feet and rushed out of Brill's office ahead of anyone else. The hallway was filled with blaring sirens, flashing red lights, and people running back and forth.

"Frank!" Joe cried out behind him. "Look!"

Ahead of him Frank saw a huge cloud of steam. It was coming down the hallway from one of the two huge rooms they'd passed on the way to Brill's office. The steam prevented Frank from being able to see clearly.

Brill stormed past Frank in the direction of the steam. Jackie George came running down the hall and grabbed Brill's arm.

"You've got a serious situation on your hands here!" she cried breathlessly.

"I'm aware of that, Jackie," Brill said, trying to move through the crowd of people gathered outside the offices. "This is an emergency situation," Brill reminded them. "Please follow evacuation procedures. Now, people. Do it."

Frank stepped through the crowd with Joe and Garth right on his heels. Next to him Frank heard a guy standing in an office doorway say to a co-worker, "I sure was hoping we'd be able to close shop without another one of these happening, weren't you?"

The co-worker nodded in agreement, then picked up some documents from her desk. "Let's get out of here, fast. I don't need to wait around to find out if this steam is irradiated!"

The two workers rushed toward the group of people trying to get to an emergency exit at the end of the hall. Frank saw that Brill didn't head for the exit, but took a left down the hall, following the source of the steam. Jackie was by his side.

"Did you hear that?" Frank turned to ask Joe.

The steam around them was getting thicker. Frank could hear some people in the crowd hollering at the emergency exit. Finally the sirens inside the plant were turned off. Still, through the steam, Frank could see flashing red lights at intervals all along the ceiling.

Joe coughed, trying to wave the steam away. "Hear what?"

"I heard it," Garth said, behind them. "Sounds

60

to me like Yankee Stalwart's had a few accidents before this one."

"Come on!" Frank urged. "I want to be there when Brill finds out what went wrong."

Frank led the way in the direction of the steam. They found Brill standing in the middle of one of the two huge, glassed-in rooms, talking loudly to a worker dressed in white coveralls. Beside them one of the huge, gleaming metal tubes was still leaking a large amount of steam from a vent at its base.

"What do you mean, it just exploded?" Brill wanted to know.

The worker held his hands out in frustration. He pushed the pair of plastic goggles he wore up over his forehead and said, "That's what happened. I was sitting at the control desk, and the vent just blew. No indication of too much pressure, no warning light on the console. Everything was fine, then, *whoosh!*" He looked somewhat sullen as he added, "Anyway, it's just steam. I mean it's not like this stuff is radioactive or anything."

"That's not the point," Brill said, obviously trying to contain his anger.

"It sure is a relief, though," Joe whispered to Frank.

"You're going to have to report this, Adam," Jackie told him. "The energy commission needs to know about it."

Brill let out a long sigh. "I realize that, Jackie."

Then the plant president caught sight of Frank,

Joe, and Garth standing nearby. "Excuse me, fellas," he said in a commanding tone, "but this is a sealed area. You guys really should have been evacuated from the plant."

"We were wondering—" Frank began.

"Later, okay?" Brill turned to the worker who stood nearby. "Hank, show these guys out for me, would you?"

Realizing that they weren't going to get anywhere with Brill, Frank let Hank escort all three of them to the emergency exit door.

In five minutes Frank, Joe, and Garth were standing outside in the Yankee Stalwart parking lot. Several plant workers were still there, even though an outdoor intercom was announcing that it was now safe to return to work.

"We sure got the brush-off," Joe said, stuffing his hands in his pockets.

"I don't think Adam Brill wanted us around while he cleaned up his mess," Garth observed.

"He sure didn't," Frank agreed.

Out of the corner of his eye Frank spotted the two workers he'd heard complaining about the accident.

"Come on," Frank said. "If Adam Brill won't talk to us, maybe some of his workers will."

Frank approached the two Yankee Stalwart employees, Joe and Garth right behind him.

"Excuse me," Frank said. "Would you mind

answering a few questions about the accident that just happened?"

The man looked at Frank skeptically, while the woman he'd been talking to shook her head and said, "No go. Yankee Stalwart employees are sworn to secrecy." She put her arms across her chest.

"We overheard you two back inside the plant," Garth pressed. "You mentioned other accidents."

The man made a surprised face. "We did?" He turned to the woman and asked her, "I don't remember that, do you?"

His co-worker just shrugged and said, "Nope. Come on, Jack. Time to get back to the old grind-stone, right?"

With that, the two employees stepped past Frank, Joe, and Garth and went back inside the plant.

Frank kicked at a rock on the ground and watched them leave. "Rats," he said, shaking his head. "I know I heard them mention accidents."

"I did, too," Garth confirmed. "So why weren't they talking?"

Joe checked his watch. "We'd better hurry if we want to sneak around Handler's place before he gets back from karate class."

The three friends got back in the van, and Garth directed Joe to David Handler's trailer. "We'll take the road that circles town," Garth said from the back seat. "David lives on the other side of Ridge City from here."

Their route took them south through the mining region. The road edged along some low, black foothills, and several times the stench of sulfur got worse.

"See that smoke?" Garth said, pointing out the site of a mine fire in the distance. "The government bored holes into the ground to ease off some of the pressure. In places it's made the fires burn out a bit. In other spots it just fueled the flames." He shook his head sadly. "The people in this town were lucky to have someone like Liz looking out for their interests."

After a ten-minute drive Garth told Joe to make a right off the main highway onto a gravel road. At the end of the road a small trailer was set in a clearing. A golden retriever started barking the minute they drove onto the road. Luckily, the dog was behind a fence that ran along the side of the trailer.

"Nice place," Joe said, pulling to a stop. "And nowhere to hide the van. We're trapped if this guy shows up."

Frank surveyed the trailer. "We'll just have to be in and out fast."

"Isn't this illegal?" Garth asked as they got out of the van.

"Not if the trailer's already open," Joe said with a smile. "Then we're just friendly visitors, only our host isn't home yet."

"Yeah, right," Garth said. "And I'm Elvis."

Frank checked the trailer's front door and found

64

it locked. He walked around to the back side and found a window there open. "Here's our way in," he called to Joe. "Give me a leg up, bro."

Joe held his palms cupped and gave Frank's foot a boost. Gripping the side of the trailer, Frank managed to squeeze into the open window. Garth then gave Joe a boost.

Leaning out the window, Frank said to Garth, "Stay there and be a lookout. Let us know if Handler drives up. We sure don't want him to catch us here."

Garth nodded, and Frank turned to look around Handler's trailer. The place was neat as a pin. On a nearby desk there were bills in even piles, and the coffee table in front of the couch had magazines arranged on it in tidy rows.

"He's going to know we searched this place," Joe said with a grimace. "There's a small bedroom in the back," he added. "I'll check it out."

Frank nodded in agreement, going over to the desk. He slid open the top drawer and saw it was filled with stationery, pens, and pencils. The drawer next to it had more office supplies, and the one below had alphabetized file folders. Frank's eyes skimmed the files. He felt his excitement rise when he spotted one with Liz's name written on it in even, block letters. Inside, Frank found a bunch of letters Handler must have gotten from Liz.

"What a weird guy," Frank said to himself. "He even files his love letters."

There were also a few that David had written to her. "Strange," Frank said aloud.

"What is?" Joe asked, appearing from the bedroom.

"There are letters here that David Handler wrote to Liz Trimmer. But apparently he never mailed them." Frank held up a letter.

" 'I can't stand this anymore,' " Frank read aloud. " 'You make me want to kill you sometimes, Liz Trimmer, as much as I love you.' "

Joe grabbed the letter from Frank and skimmed it quickly. "It's a death threat!" he cried.

"Looks like it," Frank agreed. "This guy is really creepy, Joe. He writes Liz that letter, then puts it in a file with her name on it."

"Really weird." Joe handed the letter back to Frank. "Should we stay here and confront him?"

Frank thought for a moment. "I don't think so. We still don't have any evidence. Maybe Handler was against Liz's activism. Maybe it was just some argument between the two of them."

"Maybe there are still too many *maybes*," Joe put in.

"Exactly." Frank took a last look around Handler's place, then put the folder back in the file drawer. "Let's get out of here while the coast is still clear."

"Frank! Joe!" Garth's harsh whisper floated into the trailer. "Handler's just pulled into the driveway. Get out, fast!"

Frank heard the sound of tires on gravel. Right after that the dog started barking.

"Come on," Frank urged Joe.

The younger Hardy didn't need any encouragement. Joe was already halfway out the window, his legs flying in midair as he tried to pull himself through.

Frank gave Joe a push and waited for his brother to twist free. On the other side of the trailer, Frank heard the sound of Handler's car door shut, then his footsteps coming toward the front door.

"Hurry!" Frank whispered.

"I'm trying," Joe shot back. "I think I'm stuck. Give me another push."

Frank pushed. Finally Joe fell through the window. Frank was just about to climb up himself, when he heard the front door to the trailer burst open.

Frank spun around. Handler was standing in the doorway. And the man did not look at all happy to see him.

8 Into the Mines

"You want to explain just what you're doing here?" Handler demanded. "Or should I assume you're a crook and take proper action?"

To prove his point, Handler arranged himself into a karate position.

Frank held his hands up, prepared to defend himself. There was no telling what this guy was capable of! "I can explain," Frank said in a soothing voice.

"Sure you can," Handler said. With that he swiped the air with his hands and shot a kick out in Frank's direction.

"Hey!" Frank cried, ducking. "Take it easy."

Handler spun around, prepared to deliver another blow. "Easy, eh? I find you in my house, and I'm supposed to take it easy? Right."

The man made a quick jab upward with his foot, and Frank felt a rush of air on his cheek. "Tell me why you're here, then maybe I'll take it easy," Handler growled.

Frank was in a bind. Handler stood between him and the door, and there was no way Frank would be able to scramble through the window. Frank could try to defend himself and knock the guy out, but he thought it was smarter to try to bluff his way out first.

"Remember my brother, Joe?" Frank asked. "Remember how he made an appointment to see you later this afternoon?"

Handler laughed. "Oh, please! An appointment is one thing. Breaking into my place is another. Give me a break!" Handler stood back, poised to strike again.

"Okay, okay," Frank admitted. "We came in through that open window. My brother and I were hoping we'd find a note from Liz, or some other evidence that would explain where she went."

"Don't you think I'd give you that evidence if I had it?" Handler asked. Finally the man let his hands rest at his side. Handler seemed to be calming down at the mention of Liz.

"Don't you think I want to find her, to find out what happened to her?" Handler demanded. "I love her."

69

Frank eyed the man carefully. It sounded as if he was telling the truth, but then Frank remembered how Handler hadn't stuck up for Liz during the city council meeting. Frank also thought of the note he and Joe had just found. There was still reason to suspect David Handler. But at least now it looked as if Frank would be able to leave the trailer without being turned into karate juice.

Someone started pounding on the trailer's front door. Handler went to answer it. Frank spotted Garth and Joe standing there, concerned expressions on their faces.

"Is everything okay?" Joe wanted to know.

Handler moved away from the door, and Garth and Joe peered inside. Both of them were obviously relieved to see that Frank was okay. Meanwhile, Frank realized that now was as good a time as any to beat a retreat.

"Listen," he said to Handler. "I'm really sorry that we just sneaked in like this. No hard feelings, huh? Maybe we'll come back later to ask you those questions."

Handler scowled. "If I catch you sneaking around here again—"

"Don't worry. We'll leave you alone now," Joe said hastily. He beckoned to Frank. "Come on. Garth's starving."

"I sure am," Garth put in. He grabbed Frank's arm and dragged him out of the trailer.

As the Hardys climbed back into the van, Frank

spotted Handler standing in the doorway of his trailer.

"I still get the weirdest feeling from that guy," Frank said, observing Handler in the rearview mirror as he drove.

"You're not the only one," Joe chimed in. "But we still don't have any proof that he could be the one responsible for Liz's disappearance."

"True," Frank agreed. "He still insists he wants to find her." He briefly told Garth and Joe about what had happened in the trailer before they showed up.

"Does he think we suspect him?" Garth asked.

Frank made the turn onto the highway and shook his head slowly. "He must after what just happened. If he did have something to do with the fact that Liz is missing, he's going to be watching every move we make from now on. That's for sure."

"So how about that burger?" Joe asked.

Since there didn't seem to be anything more to do that day, Frank agreed they might as well continue the investigation in the morning.

After a dinner of burgers and fries at the Ridge City Restaurant, the three friends stopped off at the video store to rent a movie. Back at the Trimmer house Frank called the sheriff. A quick check with the dispatcher told Frank that the sheriff was home for the night, and that there were no new leads in the case.

After that, Frank remembered to put a call in to

71

Con Riley. They still hadn't heard from the Bayport police detective about the results of the lab tests. Frank left a message on Con's answering machine. Then he joined Joe and Garth in the living room. "Nothing," he said in response to Garth's questioning look.

"What's going to happen?" Garth said, rubbing his eyes wearily. "Every day we don't find her is one more day I think something terrible has happened."

Joe tried to reassure their friend. "Don't think that way," he urged. "We'll find her."

"Tomorrow, I'm going to have a serious talk with Sheriff Radford," Frank said. "I think we all deserve to know exactly what he's doing to find your sister."

The next morning Joe was up before Frank or Garth. He found some juice in the refrigerator and poured himself a glass. Then he took the note Garth had gotten in the mail, the flier someone had left for him, and the map they found taped to the underside of Liz's desk. Joe spread out the evidence on the kitchen table and started trying to put together a theory—any kind of theory—that would explain what had happened to Liz Trimmer.

Joe was staring at the three pieces of evidence when Frank came into the kitchen, rubbing the sleep from his eyes.

"I just remembered we're supposed to go to that lunch meeting at Yankee Stalwart today," Frank said. "What're you up to?"

"Trying to put two and two together and not come up with five," Joe said absently. "We've got the ransom note, the flier, and then the map. The handwriting is different on each one. The kidnapper hasn't sent another note, so who knows if Liz was kidnapped at all? This map is really strange," Joe said, holding it up. "Why would Liz leave Garth a map of all the underground mine trails?"

Garth entered the kitchen from the back door. His face was red and his running clothes were soaked through with sweat.

"I needed to blow stress in a major way, so I took a little run. What's up?" Garth asked, drinking juice from the carton.

"Nothing," Joe said glumly. "That's the problem."

Frank picked up the phone. "I'm calling Sheriff Radford. I want him to meet us first thing this morning and give us a face-to-face update on his end of the case."

A few minutes later Frank had made an appointment to see Radford at the diner. Half an hour after that, Joe, Garth, and Frank were sitting in a booth, giving their orders to Angela. Joe spotted a guy sitting at the counter who looked familiar. Then he realized who it was.

73

"Hey, guys," Joe said, elbowing Frank. "Isn't that the reporter guy? What's his name? Mauer?"

"The one we saw at Yankee Stalwart?" Garth asked. He looked over at the counter and nodded. "Yep, that's him."

"He looks a lot calmer than he was yesterday," Frank said with a laugh.

Just then, Sheriff Radford walked in. With him was his deputy, Gardner. Joe got up from the booth and said, "While you guys are talking to the sheriff, I'm going to ask Mauer a few questions."

Radford and Gardner sat down in the booth with Frank and Garth. As he walked toward Mauer, Joe heard Frank starting to ask the sheriff about the investigation.

"Excuse me," Joe said, approaching the reporter. "We met yesterday at Yankee Stalwart. Joe Hardy."

The reporter looked at Joe oddly for a few moments, then seemed to recognize him. "Sure. You're looking into Liz's disappearance, right?"

"That's right." Joe indicated the seat to Mauer's left. "Mind if I sit down and ask you a few questions?"

"No problem," Mauer said, taking a sip of coffee.

"How did you know about Liz Trimmer and her disappearance?" Joe asked.

Mauer ran his hands through his hair. "I read a police bulletin about it. But I knew about Liz before I heard she'd disappeared."

74

"You did?" Joe placed his elbows on the counter. "How was that?"

"She contacted me by mail," Mauer said. "We wrote several letters back and forth. I knew she'd gotten involved in some kind of investigation connected to the government proposal here in Ridge City."

"Something to do with Yankee Stalwart?" Joe guessed.

"Exactly. That's how I knew about Brill." Mauer paused and blushed with embarrassment. "I'm lucky Brill didn't call the cops on me. I don't know why I lost my head out there yesterday, but I did. It's just that I liked Liz a lot, and I had a lot of respect for what she was trying to do for the people here in Ridge City. I told Liz I was going to write an in-depth profile on her once this was all over."

Joe thought for a minute. "You were in touch with her. Do you know what she was investigating at Yankee Stalwart? Do you have any ideas what might have happened to her? Do you think someone kidnapped her?"

"Hey! One question at a time!" Mauer laughed. "Liz wouldn't say a word about what she was looking into out at the plant. I think she had some suspicions but wanted to collect proof before she said anything outright."

"Proof of what?" Joe asked, frustrated.

"Who knows? Bad bookkeeping? Bad management?"

"Maybe accidents?" Joe suggested. He thought about what Frank had heard the Yankee Stalwart employees discussing the day before.

Mauer shrugged. "Could be. As far as kidnapping goes—" The reporter narrowed his eyes. "I think she was in danger, but I don't think that much danger. Besides, I got a weird message from her a few days before she disappeared."

"What kind of message?" Joe asked.

Mauer lowered his voice. "I think I can trust you. She said she was going underground. She said she'd resurface in a few days, and that by then she hoped to have the proof she needed."

Joe's thoughts went a mile a minute. "What you're telling me is that you think Liz Trimmer disappeared voluntarily. That she wasn't kidnapped at all!"

"Exactly," Mauer said, his voice barely a whisper. "And I think Brill knows more than he's letting on. Why do you think I'm still hanging around?"

Over at their booth Gardner and the sheriff were getting up from Frank and Garth's table. Joe tried to make sense of what Mauer had told him. Suddenly he thought about the mine map taped to the underside of Liz's desk.

"That's it!" Joe cried. "Thanks!" he called out to Mauer as he rushed over to the booth where Frank and Garth were still sitting. "We've got to check the tunnels!" Joe cried, grabbing Frank's arm. "Come on."

76

They were out the door before Joe could explain to Frank what was on his mind. The sheriff was still standing outside.

"Sheriff Radford!" Joe cried breathlessly. "Have you checked the mine tunnels for any sign of Liz Trimmer?"

The sheriff took off his cap, scratched his bald head, and gave Joe a confused look. "Now, wouldn't that be one of the first places I'd look, son?" he asked.

"I guess so," Joe admitted.

"Do you want to explain what's going on?" Frank asked.

Joe quickly told his brother and Garth what Mauer had said about Liz going underground. "I think it means she's down inside the mines," Joe said with enthusiasm. "Think about it: the map, then this. We've got our first big lead!"

Frank's eyes went wide. "I'm not sure, Joe," he said skeptically. "Why would she go down there? It's dangerous, and there's no light or air."

Garth stood by. When Joe asked him what he thought, Garth said, "I guess it's worth a try. Let's go."

Before they could leave, the sheriff put his hand on Joe's arm. "What's this about a map?" he asked.

Joe handed the map over to the sheriff and explained how Liz had left it for Garth.

"So it wasn't with those books your sister sent you," the sheriff concluded, looking the map over.

Garth shook his head. "Nope. It was waiting for us when I got here."

The sheriff looked at Garth for a moment, then gave the map back to Joe.

"That's a common surveyor's map," he said. "Nothing unusual or mysterious about it. I don't even think it's a real lead, if you ask me. But if you boys want to search the mines, we'll do it. I'll meet you up at the mine office. That's where all the trails lead off from, so we can spread out from there."

"Sounds good," Joe said excitedly.

Frank drove, and Garth gave directions. On their way to the abandoned mine offices, Joe studied the map.

"The sheriff's wrong about this map," Joe said, noticing small notations in pencil on each one of the trails. "There are little check marks here on some of the underground tunnels. Others don't have them. What do you think, Garth?"

"The checks could be indicating which tunnels have fires, I suppose. I really don't know."

Frank turned into a run-down drive. Up ahead, Joe spotted several brick buildings in disrepair. Weeds grew between cracks in the parking lot. Several windows in the mine's offices were broken. A shaft built into a hillside was falling down, and a pile of dirt blocked the entrance.

"It's been a little while since this place was used," Frank observed.

78

"Eight years, to be exact," Garth informed him. "That's how long the fires have been out of control."

Frank parked the van. They had arrived before the sheriff. Joe leaped from the van and started walking rapidly toward one of the abandoned buildings. Frank and Garth followed right behind him.

"I'll take the building on the left," Joe said. "Why don't you guys search the one over there." He pointed to a similar brick building closer to the abandoned shaft. "Liz may be using this place for shelter if she's searching underground in the mines."

Joe was about to climb through a broken window when he noticed the front door to the building was already wide open. Joe stepped inside and immediately felt a spiderweb across his face. Luckily, there was enough light from all the broken windows for him to see his way around.

Downstairs, the building was a series of rooms, each one filled with trash and debris. There was no sign that anyone had been hiding out there, though, so Joe went up the rickety steps to the second floor. There, he found a bathroom and more, smaller rooms. In one of them there was a row of lockers, all without locks.

Joe went over to the lockers and started searching them. The first few were empty—except for a lot of dust. Then Joe's eyes fell on a locker that looked as if it had fresh fingerprints on its dusty green surface.

Joe yanked the door open, and his eyes went wide with surprise at what he saw. The locker was filled with canned food, boxes of cereal, and plastic jugs of water.

His hunch had been right. Liz Trimmer really was hiding out in the mines!

9 Cave-in!

"Frank!" Joe called out, rushing back downstairs. "Garth! I think I found something."

Frank and Garth came running out of the building across the way. "What?" Frank asked breathlessly.

"There's a stash of food in a locker upstairs," Joe told him. "I bet you anything it belongs to Liz."

Joe led Frank and Garth back inside the building and upstairs to where the lockers were. When Frank saw the cans of food and the bottles of water, he stopped dead in his tracks. Garth eagerly reached for one of the cereal boxes, but Joe stopped him.

"We'll want to dust for prints," Joe warned. "You

shouldn't touch anything." Using the end of his shirt to carefully remove one of the cans, he gingerly put it in his pocket. "We brought our fingerprinting kit along. I'll dust this can when we get back to your house."

Garth nodded excitedly. "No problem." He pointed to the box of cereal. "I guess I got carried away. That's Liz's favorite granola."

"Bingo," Joe said, his excitement rising. "She's been here, I'm sure of it."

"Finally we're getting somewhere," Garth said, a smile lighting his face for the first time in days.

"Finding this food pretty much kills the kidnapping angle," Frank admitted. "It seems unlikely that someone would abduct Liz and then lay in a stash of her favorite food."

"Radford owes us an explanation about how and why he didn't find this locker," Joe remarked.

"The sheriff says he searched these buildings," Garth said. "And the tunnels running underground from here. Back at the diner he told me and Frank he's convinced Liz left town—on her own, and voluntarily. He's about to give up his investigation." Garth pounded his fist against the lockers in a burst of anger. "I can't believe him! If Liz left town, why did she stash this food? I think he just doesn't care about finding her. That's what I think."

Frank looked troubled. "There's another possibility—one we haven't thought about yet," he said slowly. "We have to consider that maybe Sheriff Radford doesn't want us to find Liz."

Joe had been poking through another locker. He froze as he realized what his brother was suggesting. "You mean Radford could have had something to do with Liz's disappearance?" he asked, straightening up.

Frank nodded. "And all this time we've been telling him everything about our investigation."

"Whoa, hold on," Garth protested. "Radford may be lazy, but I can't believe he's a crook. I've known him since I was a kid!"

"There's another thing," Joe put in. "Whoever it was who came to get the notebook at the covered bridge, it sure wasn't Radford. That guy was skinny. Sheriff Radford would have made three of him."

"Hey, you're right," Frank agreed. "But he could have an accomplice. But, then again, he did send some officers to try to catch the kidnapper—even if he put them at the wrong end of the bridge." Frank was silent for a moment. Then he said, "I suppose that could have been deliberate, though."

From outside came the noise of a car door slamming. Joe crossed to the dusty window and peered down. There were two cars in front of the mine office. Sheriff Radford and Deputy Gardner stood by one, and Fred Mauer was just climbing out of the other.

"Well, Radford's here now," Joe reported. "Let's

show him the stash of food and see how he reacts."
He rapped on the windowpane and beckoned vigorously. "Up here!" he shouted. "We have something to show you."

The sheriff came lumbering up the stairs. Gardner was with him, and Mauer was fast on their trail. Joe opened the locker with a flourish, and the sheriff almost fell over in surprise.

If he's acting, Joe thought, he should be in the movies.

"Well . . . I'll be." The sheriff stood with his mouth gaping for a moment. "None of this was here when my men and I searched these buildings two days ago," Radford said. "I guess you boys think the kidnapper bought this stuff for Liz."

"No, we don't," Joe said contemptuously. "We're beginning to think Liz Trimmer wasn't kidnapped at all."

"Really?" Deputy Gardner said. "What about that little note you fellas got back in Bayport?"

The sheriff smiled at Gardner. "Now, don't give these guys a hard time, especially when they're coming over to my side."

Radford sat down on the edge of a nearby brokendown bench and rubbed his eyes wearily. "Here are the facts," he said. "You kids never got another ransom note, and you don't know what the notebook was that the kidnapper demanded."

"So Liz wasn't kidnapped," Frank said in exasperation.

"But what about that note?" the sheriff pressed. "Why did some stranger demand a notebook from you? What was that all about?"

"We don't know," Garth said. "We've told you. I got a couple of books on mining from my sister in the mail a few days earlier, but no notebook."

Radford looked at Garth curiously, then let out a deep sigh. "Let's say the kidnapping was a complete hoax. Weird, but a hoax. Why did your sister disappear?"

Before Garth could say a word, the sheriff answered his own question. "Because she's a kook— no offense, Garth. But look at that guy she goes with—Handler. Anyway, that doesn't change the fact that she left this food and we still have to look for her."

With that, the sheriff stood up again and walked across the room toward the stairs. "Come on, Gardner. We've got to search the tunnels underneath this place one more time. I'm calling all my men over here," Radford told the Hardys and Garth. "I'll give this investigation another two days. After that, I'm going to assume Liz Trimmer left town willingly, and voluntarily. Period."

Joe watched the sheriff leave with his deputy in tow. As the men went downstairs, Mauer came forward. "I told you Liz stuck around!" the reporter said with conviction. He took out his pad and furiously started scribbling notes. "We're going to get to the bottom of this."

"I sure hope so," Joe said as Mauer peeked inside the locker. Joe's hand found the mine map where he'd put it inside his jacket pocket. He removed the map and spread it across the bench. He studied the tunnels while Frank and Garth peered over his shoulder.

"See how some of these trails are checked off with a pencil mark?" Joe said, pointing.

Frank nodded. "Let's start searching the tunnels that aren't checked off. I get the feeling Liz was looking for something in these tunnels. She might still be searching in the trails that are unmarked."

"Okay, okay," Garth said, following Frank's finger. "But searching for what? We still don't know the answer to that." Frank could tell that Garth was anxious to get moving.

Mauer leaned in. "I just know it's got something to do with that government proposal," he said. "Maybe the mine fires. Maybe she found evidence that the destruction is even worse than people thought."

Joe considered the reporter's theory. "Could be. But why would she have to go underground to do that? Liz could have searched the tunnels in broad daylight, to her heart's content. Why fake a disappearance?"

"We won't know a thing until we find her," Frank said, grabbing the map from the bench. "Let's split up. There are still lots of tunnels that haven't been searched. Joe and I can take one. Garth, you and Mauer can take another. When the sheriff's men get here, we can come back out and direct them to the others."

Within five minutes Frank and Joe were on their way into an elevator that would take them down into the tunnels. Garth and Mauer were at their heels.

The elevator was creaky but still worked. Joe cranked the gears that lowered it, and after descending at least fifty feet, he stopped the car at the bottom. They stepped out of the elevator to discover they were in a spot where all the trails split off.

"It's like spokes on a wheel," Frank pointed out, "and we're at the hub." He checked the map, then directed Garth and Mauer to a tunnel off to the right. "You guys take that one. Joe and I will follow this other one. Let's meet back here in"—Frank checked his watch—"half an hour?"

Mauer nodded and flicked on the flashlight Joe had given him. The reporter started down the tunnel Frank had pointed out.

"Be careful," Garth warned as Frank and Joe set off. "These shafts can be dangerous. If you smell sulfur, or smoke, you could be near an underground fire. Turn around and get out right away."

"How do you know so much about the mines?" Joe asked.

"Hey, I've been reading the books Liz sent me," Garth said with a wide grin.

The beam from Frank's flashlight cast an eerie glow on the inside of the tunnel. Joe pushed aside spiderwebs above their heads. Both Hardys had to bend over to avoid hitting the beams along the roof of the tunnel.

They walked for what felt to Joe like miles. The shaft grew blacker, and lower, until finally it ended.

"Just like this case," Frank said, eyeing the wall of coal in front of them. "Another dead end."

"Let's head back," Joe said. "There are still more tunnels to search."

Frank led the way back out of the tunnel. After several minutes Joe spied with relief a small beam of light at the end. Even though he knew they still had many more tunnels to search, he'd be glad to get some fresh air. Inside the shaft there was so much dust and dirt, it was hard to breathe.

Just then one of the beams overhead creaked ominously.

"What was that?" Frank called out, turning around. The older Hardy used his flashlight to play along the ceiling of the shaft. The beam that had made the noise was perilously close to splintering apart.

"Joe!" Frank called out. "Hurry!"

The beam was between Joe and Frank. Joe tried to leap out of the way, just as huge clumps of coal started to fall from above.

"Grab my hand!" Frank shouted desperately,

groping for his brother through the downpour of black debris.

But it was too late. The beam broke apart, splintering into several pieces. The shaft's ceiling gave way entirely. More coal came falling from above, and the walls started caving in, too.

Joe Hardy was about to be buried alive!

10 Buried Alive

Frank Hardy watched in horror as his younger brother disappeared behind a mound of coal.

"Joe!" Frank yelled.

Behind him, Frank heard footsteps running into the tunnel. He turned to see Deputy Gardner and another officer.

"What's going on?" Gardner demanded.

"My brother's behind that wall of coal!" Frank said frantically. "We've got to save him before this cave-in sets off another!"

All along the roof of the shaft Frank heard other beams creaking. Coal still fell like rain up and down the tunnel. Falling to his knees, Frank began scraping frantically at the pile of rubble.

"Hold on, son." Deputy Gardner caught Frank's arm. "Don't make it worse! We're going to need a rescue crew down here."

Frank crouched by the cave-in while Gardner and the other officer ran out. He stared helplessly at the huge mound of coal in front of him, knowing there was nothing he could do on his own. He called his brother's name twice, but there was no answer.

Moments later Gardner returned. Garth and Mauer were right behind him.

"We heard what happened," Garth said. "Man. I hope Joe's okay back there."

Frank swallowed hard. He had been trying not to think about what might have happened to Joe. "We've got to get to him," he said.

"The rescue crew's on its way," Gardner told him. "We'll get your brother out of there."

Ten long minutes later Frank stepped aside as workers entered the tunnel carrying shovels, wheel-barrows, and pieces of wood. Several of the men propped the two-by-fours into the ceiling to stop the shaft from caving in again. Then the others started digging away at the pile.

"They seem to know what they're doing," Frank said, observing the men.

Gardner nodded. "When the mine was still operational, we had a lot of cave-ins up here." He shook his head. "Ridge City's a disaster area. Garth, I'm sorry about your sister disappearing, but I have to say, I think she's in the wrong. The sooner we clear this area out the happier I'll be."

Garth bristled. "Maybe that's why you all haven't really tried to find Liz, huh?" he said angrily. "She's too inconvenient."

Gardner's eyes hardened. "We are following procedure," he growled.

Too late, Frank tuned in to Garth and Gardner's conversation. He sighed, wishing Garth could keep his mouth shut. It never helped to make enemies of the police.

At that moment a worker on the rescue crew cried out. "I got him! I got him in sight!"

Frank rushed past the workers toward the mound of coal. On top of the pile one of the workers was furiously digging away. Frank scrambled to the top and put his head up to the space the worker had cleared.

Shining his flashlight toward the ground, Frank made out his brother through the soot-filled air. Joe Hardy lay at the bottom of the other side of the mound. He was pale and still, but Frank could see him breathing. A serious bruise was forming on his forehead.

"We've got to hurry," Frank said. "He's in trouble."

Frank helped the worker dig away at the pile. Finally they had cleared enough space for Frank to crawl through. He stumbled down the side to his brother.

92

Joe was just coming to as Frank reached him. "What happened?" he asked, sitting up slowly. Then he felt his forehead and grimaced. "Ouch."

"The shaft caved in," Frank said. "Can you stand up?"

"I think so," Joe said. "I'm just a little wobbly."

Frank helped Joe to his feet, then got behind his brother and pushed him up the pile of coal.

"Go easy," Joe groaned. "I've just seen my life pass before my eyes, and I'm still recovering."

With a little help Frank managed to get Joe up and over the mound of coal. When Garth saw him emerge on the other side, he let out a howl of relief. "All right! Joe Hardy lives!"

Joe smiled weakly, his face a mask of black soot. Frank helped his brother into the elevator and cranked the car up out of the mines. When they made it to the top, the fresh air was a relief. So was the sight of half a dozen squad cars.

"It looks as if Radford's finally taking us seriously," Joe said.

Garth tapped Frank on the shoulder. "Don't forget we've got a meeting at Yankee Stalwart," he reminded him.

Frank looked at Joe in concern. "Do you feel up for it? I'm thinking we should get you to a hospital."

Joe touched the bump on his forehead. "I've been conked out before, Frank. It didn't stop me then, and it's not going to stop me now. Let's go. You coming with us, Mauer?"

The reporter shook his head no. "I'm not exactly welcome there, remember? I think I'll stick around here and see if they find anything else."

Mauer handed his business card to Frank. "You guys call me if you get anywhere. Or if you have any questions. I'm staying at a motel back by the interstate. The number's on the bottom of the card."

"Thanks," Frank said. The three friends waved goodbye to Mauer and headed for the van. Frank got in on the driver's side, while Garth took the passenger seat, and Joe stretched out in the back.

Garth gave Frank instructions on how to take the northern route that bypassed town. It was a quick ten-minute drive to the plant. They stopped at a gas station so Joe could wash up and drink a soda. Back on the road Frank saw the smoke from several underground fires, along with the boreholes cut into the ground to ease some of the pressure.

They parked the van in the visitor lot of Yankee Stalwart and went around to the front entrance. Frank told Hetty, the receptionist, that they were there for the meeting. She called Brill's secretary out to show them back to the conference room where the meeting was to take place.

When they got to the conference room, they were

94

shocked to see David Handler sitting at the table. The man looked surprised to see them, too. As Garth and the Hardys entered the room, Handler was chatting easily with the mayor, who was also there. For a moment David stopped his conversation and stared at Frank.

"Nice to see you, Dave," Frank said, giving Handler a wave.

David sank into his chair and gave the Hardys and Garth a suspicious look. Adam Brill entered the conference room, sat down, and called the meeting to order.

"You all know one another, I think." Brill introduced Jackie George, Mayor Stephenson, and David Handler to Frank, Joe, and Garth. Several other city council members were also there, along with other Yankee Stalwart executives.

Brill read from the notes in front of him. "We have two items on the agenda today. First, we need to go over some procedural and legal points regarding the shutdown of Yankee Stalwart. Second, we're here to discuss the fine points of the government's generous proposal to buy out property owners and residents of Ridge City." Brill looked around the room with raised eyebrows. "I believe we're all very much in favor of it."

Beside him, Frank heard Garth cough loudly.

Brill turned to Garth. "Is there something wrong?" he asked.

Frank eyed his friend. Garth's lips were pressed together, as if he was trying not to say something. Finally he blurted out, "I can't sit here and listen to you go through with something I know my sister was against. I know she can't be here to defend herself, so I have to."

"Garth," Joe said under his breath. "This isn't the time—"

"I know, I know." Garth turned to Brill. "This is my idea, not theirs. You were nice to invite us here. I don't mean to be rude, but I have reason to suspect my sister was on the track of hard evidence. Evidence that would mean the government was offering Ridge City way too little money."

"What kind of evidence?" Brill asked through narrowed eyes.

Frank saw Handler shift uncomfortably in his seat. "We really don't have time for this," David said.

Garth let out a deep breath. "We don't know what my sister was investigating, that's the problem. But we're getting closer—"

"Oh, please," said the mayor, speaking up for the first time. "I've had just about enough of this from Liz Trimmer's friends and family. I'm prepared to go ahead."

Garth fidgeted in his seat. "You can't do this," he muttered.

"I most certainly can, young man." The mayor

drew herself up in her seat and pursed her lips. "In fact, I'm prepared to say so right here and now."

Mayor Stephenson tapped the stack of papers in front of her. "I'm going to put this proposal to a vote in two days," she announced. "After that, Liz Trimmer won't be able to have any say whatsoever in the future of this town!"

11 Running Out of Time

Joe Hardy couldn't believe his ears. "You mean to say that unless Liz Trimmer turns up to object, you'll go ahead with this proposal?" he said.

Garth jumped up from his seat. The chair he'd been sitting in toppled to the ground. "That's unfair!" he cried.

"That's democracy, young man," the mayor said, looking at Garth with her cool green eyes. "The proposal has been on the table for months. So has the date of the vote. In all that time Liz Trimmer hasn't been able to find anything to back up all her wild ideas. She had her chance. We've had the public discussion. Now it's time to vote. Unless I'm wrong, the council will approve the proposal. And then," Stephenson said, nodding to Brill, "I will sign it."

Brill smiled at the mayor, then stood up and put a reassuring hand on Garth's arm. "Young man, I'm sorry about your sister, but I'm sure you do understand."

"No, I don't!" Garth cried in frustration. His face was red and his fists were clenched at his side. Joe really felt for his friend. "All I know is I was right when I said this town stinks. And it's not just the sulfur that's making it smell."

With that, Garth rushed from the room. Frank and Joe looked at each other, trying to decide what they should do. Joe was torn. As much as he wanted to follow Garth, he also wanted to stay for the rest of the meeting. Something important might turn up.

Finally Frank motioned to Joe that he would go after Garth. "You stay here," Frank whispered to Joe as he got up to go. "We'll wait for you in the parking lot."

Unfortunately, the rest of the meeting was uneventful. Brill presented the plans for shutting down the plant. Jackie George ran down the list of government procedures Yankee Stalwart would have to follow to close down. The mayor took notes and nodded.

Meanwhile, David Handler just sat in his seat, silently watching what went on. Joe badly wanted to know what was going on in Handler's mind.

Finally the meeting was ending, and Joe crossed the room to where Handler sat.

"By the way," Joe said casually. "We have reason to think that Liz Trimmer wasn't kidnapped, and that she didn't have an accident."

Handler's eyes went wide. "You do?" he stammered.

"That's right." Joe told the man about the stash of food he'd found up at the mine offices. "We've got a new theory."

"Which is?" Handler asked. He licked his lips and nervously straightened the pile of papers in front of him without looking at Joe.

"We think she disappeared voluntarily."

"Don't be ridiculous," Handler snapped. "That's just not like Liz."

"You don't sound very happy about this development," Joe said. "I'd think you'd be excited to find this out. That is, unless you don't want her to come back."

"What?" Handler stood up suddenly and assumed a threatening stance. "I don't like what you're saying."

"Maybe you hope Liz stays away until the proposal is passed," Joe said.

"I'm not even going to answer that!" Handler snapped in disgust.

The mayor turned their way, and Handler reached out to shake her hand. After that he gave Joe a nasty look and slipped out of the room.

Joe watched him leave in frustration. The guy definitely had something to do with Liz's disappearance. He was sure of it. But what? And why?

And then there was the mayor. Joe observed Lucy Stephenson carefully as she said her goodbyes—her neat suit and her perfectly styled hair. Could she be ambitious enough to have threatened Liz Trimmer? It occurred to Joe that maybe Liz Trimmer had received some serious threats from someone—either the mayor or Handler. Liz might have gone underground to find the evidence she was looking for, but also to avoid danger.

Brill left, along with the mayor and Handler. Jackie George was collecting her papers. On a hunch Joe went over to her and asked, "What if I told you Liz Trimmer was collecting information against Yankee Stalwart?"

The government official looked at Joe skeptically. "Then I'd tell you that you were making a serious charge."

"Say it was information about other accidents here at Yankee Stalwart," Joe said, thinking about the conversation Frank overheard at the plant the day before. "Would that kind of information affect this proposal?"

"You bet it would. But there would be an investigation first." Jackie narrowed her eyes and held her papers under her arm.

"If this turns out to be the case," Jackie continued, "you will of course notify me. No matter what Adam Brill says, this plant needs to close down in the cleanest and most efficient way possible. I'm here to make sure that happens, and that we don't cut corners. Now, if you'll excuse me . . ." With that she left the room.

Joe followed her out and made his way back through the plant. Within a few minutes he was back at the van, reporting on what he'd learned.

"I can't figure all this out," Joe said. "My head's swimming, trying to process everything. There's Handler, and the mayor, and the possibility that either one of them threatened Liz, forcing her into hiding."

"My vote's on Handler," Frank said, starting up the van.

"But then there's the evidence angle," Joe said. "What exactly was Liz looking for?"

Garth sighed heavily. "I'm beginning to wonder if we'll ever find out."

There was a gloomy silence. Then Frank started the van.

"Where to?" he asked.

Joe thought for a moment. "I want to dust that can we took from the locker for fingerprints. My guess is we'll just find Liz's prints, but who knows? Then I want to call Mauer and pick his brain about the Yankee Stalwart angle."

"I hope I can finally get in touch with Con

Riley," Frank said, taking a turn onto the highway in the direction of Garth's house.

"Hey, I'm sorry I lost my temper back there," Garth said from the back seat. "I hope I didn't blow it."

"Nah," Joe said. "But next time you want to throw around your two hundred and fifty pounds of solid muscle, wait for the gym, okay?"

Garth laughed. "Okay," he said softly. "It's a deal."

Ten minutes later Frank was pulling into Garth's driveway. Joe was startled to see the curtain billowing out from the living room window.

"Hey, did we leave that window open?" he asked.

"Maybe," Garth said, getting out of the van. "I don't remember."

Slowly Joe walked up the steps to the front porch. "I must be paranoid," he said, reaching for the doorknob and finding it locked. "I keep expecting crime to stick to us like a bad smell."

"Chill out," Frank urged while Garth took out his key and unlocked the front door. "We've already got enough unsolved mysteries on our hands. We don't need to invent more."

"Right." Joe followed Garth and Frank inside.

Garth went straight back to the kitchen, saying, "I'm thirsty. You guys want some water or juice or something?"

"No, thanks," Frank said. "I'll get the dusting kit," he told Joe. Then he ran upstairs, taking the steps two at a time.

Joe strolled into the living room. And what he saw confirmed his worst suspicions. The window was wide open, and the room was in shambles.

Someone had broken in and ransacked Garth Trimmer's house.

12 Another Break-in

"Frank! Someone broke into the house!" Joe called out.

Frank grabbed the fingerprinting kit from his duffel bag and raced down the hall. As he was about to head downstairs, he saw that the door to Garth's room was open.

"Hold on a sec!" Frank cried, rushing into Garth's bedroom.

The place was a mess. Everything had been pulled from Garth's duffel bag and thrown across the floor. There were books and tapes everywhere. Someone had even ripped the pages from one of Garth's books and scattered them on the floor.

Frank let out a deep breath, then headed downstairs. Joe was standing in the hallway, along with Garth.

"The living room is all torn up," Joe said.

"Same with Garth's room," Frank confirmed.

Garth pounded his fist into a wall. "Not again! What's this person looking for? And why does he think I have it?"

"My guess is this," Frank said, sitting down on the bottom step. "Someone thinks Liz sent you information."

"What kind of information?" Garth asked.

"Something connected to whatever Liz was investigating," Frank said.

Joe nodded. "You've got to be right." The younger Hardy started pacing up and down the hall, talking as he went. "Liz was looking for evidence— maybe about the accidents at Yankee Stalwart, maybe about the government proposal. Someone knew that, and Liz realized she was in danger because of it."

"So she went underground," Frank added. "But before she did, she sent you those books."

"But that's totally unrelated," Garth said. "I mean, I agree the timing's right. Still, there's nothing in those books that has to do with either the proposal or Yankee Stalwart."

"Sure," Frank said, thinking hard. "But whoever is looking for that evidence doesn't know that. All that person knows is that he—or she—saw Liz sending you something in the mail. And then Liz disappeared."

"Well, this is just great," Garth said. He rubbed his eyes and said quietly, "Some goon is looking for something I don't have. And he's probably getting pretty mad that he can't find it. Terrific. Just what I need."

"There's one good thing in all this," Joe said, looking up at Frank.

"What's that?" Frank asked.

Joe grinned from ear to ear. "When we find the guy who keeps messing around with Garth's stuff, we'll also find the guy who made Liz go into hiding."

"That's right!" Frank practically cried out.

"Hey, don't get all excited. My idea wasn't that brilliant," Joe said.

Frank leapt up from where he was sitting. "You're wrong, Joe. It was." Frank rubbed his chin thoughtfully. "That's the connection we've been looking for. So what do we know about the break-ins?"

"The guy who broke into my house had a dog," Garth reminded them. "Remember the orange hairs?"

"David Handler has a dog, a golden retriever," Joe said softly.

"Handler!" Frank and Garth cried at once.

Frank rushed into the living room and got down on his hands and knees to search the floor. Within a few seconds he'd found at least three golden dog hairs, all the same kind as the ones they'd discovered at Garth's apartment back in Bayport.

Holding the dog hair between a pair of tweezers, Frank said, "Is this enough evidence to have the sheriff call Handler in for questioning?"

"You bet it is," Joe said with enthusiasm. "I always knew there was something sneaky about that guy."

Frank went into the kitchen and called the sheriff. He quickly told Radford about their suspicions, and the sheriff agreed to send some men out to Handler's trailer to pick him up.

"In the meantime," the sheriff said, "I should tell you that I'm calling my men back in from the mines for the day."

"What?" Frank asked, stunned. "After we found that food and everything?"

"Son, we have searched as much as we can in one day." The sheriff sighed in exhaustion. "My men are dead tired. I only have four officers, you know, and there are miles and miles of tunnel. They've got to take a break, get some rest!"

Frank gritted his teeth in frustration. "So you don't care that Liz Trimmer could be in danger? That whoever sent Garth the ransom note is probably searching for her just like we are—if they haven't already caught her? That doesn't worry you?"

"I am doing my best, son," the sheriff objected. "I can't do any more."

Frank felt himself cooling down. Maybe the sheriff was right. Maybe he was doing his best.

"I'm sorry, Sheriff," Frank said. "It's just that we need to find Liz. The mayor says she's going to sign that proposal in two days, if the council approves. And we think Liz has a reason for vetoing it. After the vote it will be too late."

The sheriff let out a long sigh. "Listen. Why don't you boys pick up the search tonight? Take the longest tunnel, the one that goes to Yankee Stalwart. We haven't had a chance to search there yet, or the other long one that heads in the direction of the high school. I'll give my men some rest and have them start early tomorrow on the others. Deal?"

"It's a deal," Frank agreed. "I'll call you if I find anything. And let me know what happens with Handler." Frank gave Radford the number at Garth's and hung up.

Joe and Garth came into the kitchen. "I've dusted the can I took from the locker," Joe said. He held up a sheet of paper. "We've got four good prints here. Let's express them out to Con Riley. Even though it's late, he'll get them tomorrow and probably can have a report for us by the end of the day. If anyone who handled the can has a criminal record, it might be in the police data base, and then we'll have a good solid lead. Meanwhile, we can also leave a message with Con about the dog hair. Maybe he has a report for us."

Frank nodded, then told the two of them what he'd been discussing with Radford. "We can hunt through the tunnel after we mail the prints," Frank said. "Do you still have the mine map?"

Joe took the map from his back pocket. It was a little crumpled but still legible. "You bet I do. I've marked off the tunnels we searched earlier today."

"The sheriff said to take the one that goes to Yankee Stalwart," Frank said. "Tomorrow, the sheriff and his men will search some more."

Joe called and left a message for Con Riley, telling him that he was sending prints by express mail. After a quick dinner of grilled cheese sandwiches, the Hardys and Garth piled back in the van. Garth directed Joe, who was driving, to the nearest express office. Then the three friends doubled back and headed for the mine offices.

At night the mining complex was even creepier than it was during the day. The two abandoned buildings looked ghostly, with the dull white moonlight sending a beam of light across their broken windows.

After he parked the van, Joe grabbed two flashlights from the glove compartment and gave one to Frank. Joe studied the map. "It shouldn't be too hard to find the entrance to the tunnel that goes to Yankee Stalwart."

110

"Remember how I told you there's a wall protecting Yankee Stalwart from the fires?" Garth said. "We may run right into it."

"And another dead end," Frank joked. He pointed to the tunnel on the map. "Do you know where the mine fires start? Is this tunnel close to them?"

Garth drew in a deep breath and bit on his lower lip. "I'm just not sure. I think the fires are more to the north, and east, of this trail. But don't worry—we'll know if we're getting close. There'll be a lot of smoke, and the fumes will be intense."

"Great," said Joe, switching on his flashlight. "Let's do it."

Joe led the way inside the shaft. The Hardys took the elevator down into the mines and quickly located the entrance to the tunnel that led to Yankee Stalwart. Joe watched the beams along the ceiling. Back underground, he felt a little nervous about the last time he'd been inside the mines. Beneath their feet the narrow-gauge train tracks disappeared into the end of the tunnel.

"These tracks almost look as if they've been used," Joe observed. "Look how shiny they are, like a railcar's passed over them recently."

Frank nodded and followed Joe. Around them the black coal walls shone dimly. The tunnel got narrower and, it seemed, darker.

"How much farther?" Garth asked.

"Hard to tell," Joe said, checking the map. "There aren't exactly a lot of markers down here. Wait a minute," he said suddenly. "Hear that?"

Ahead of them, in the distance, there was a low, grinding hum. Joe heard a clicking sound, too. And they were both getting louder.

"I hear it," Frank whispered.

"It sounds like a train," Joe said, stunned.

"And it's coming this way," Garth confirmed.

Joe aimed his flashlight up ahead into the tunnel. Suddenly a blinding light rounded a bend in the tunnel.

"It *is* a train!" Joe shouted. "And it's coming right at us!"

13 Down in the Tunnels

"Joe!" Frank cried behind him. "Look out!"

The train came barreling closer. The light blinded Joe. On either side of him were the shiny black walls of the mine shaft. There was nowhere to run!

At the last minute, just before the train was about to run him down, Joe spotted a small opening in the right-hand side of the tunnel. With no time to think, he jumped over the tracks to the other side. Then he pressed himself into the wall and held his breath as the train approached. There was hardly any room, but he was safe.

With a thunderous roar the train clamored past. Joe tried to see who was manning the engine, but it was too dark. He let out his breath in a big *whoosh* of relief when he realized the coast was clear. "Too close for comfort," Joe said to himself as he looked down the tracks at the departing train.

There was no sign of Frank or Garth on the tracks. Joe's heart was pounding in his chest.

"Frank," he called out. "Garth. Where are you guys?"

Just then Frank emerged from another small opening on the other side of the tunnel. Garth appeared next to him.

"We're lucky someone built these alcoves into the side of the tracks," Frank said, letting out a deep breath. "Otherwise, we'd be chop suey right now."

"Who on earth was that guy?" Garth demanded, turning to watch the train disappear.

Joe panted and shook his head in frustration. "Who knows. But I'm sure going to find out."

Joe took off at a run, following the train. He heard Frank call out after him, then the sound of Frank's footsteps behind him. Soon Frank was running alongside Joe, and Garth was with him.

The three friends raced down the tracks. Finally they caught up with the train, which had stopped at the entrance to the tunnel.

Joe jumped into the engine car, prepared for a fight. But the car was empty, and there was no sign of the conductor.

"Don't say it, Frank," Joe muttered, staring at the empty car. "Another dead end."

"Maybe," Frank said, running his flashlight around the inside of the car. "Except—check this out." Frank bent over and picked something up from the engine car's bench seat. "Our culprit strikes again."

Frank passed a dog hair to Joe, who took it and let out a low whistle.

"What's that?" Garth wanted to know.

"David Handler," Joe said. "Our favorite dog owner was right on our track."

"But how'd he know where to find us?" Garth asked.

Joe scratched the back of his head. "Who knows? Maybe he followed us. Or maybe he just came upon us by accident. He could be down here looking for Liz."

"You don't think—" Garth began, his eyes wide.

"Don't even say it," Frank said, scanning the rest of the car with his flashlight. "It could be that Handler threatened Liz, and that's why she disappeared. He could be looking for her down here. But until the sheriff brings him in, that's nothing but a hunch."

Joe jumped from the car and walked toward the elevator. The car was up above, on the ground floor level. "That guy's long gone by now," he said, looking up. "Come on. Let's keep looking. I think we're safe for a little while."

Frank stepped off the engine car and kicked at a piece of coal on the ground. "One thing that's bothering me. Now we know why these tracks look as if they've been used. They have. But why? And for what? What has Handler been doing down here?"

The Hardys and Garth started walking down the tunnel, searching each nook and cranny for any sign that Liz had been there. Joe managed to forget about the train that had nearly run them over. He even managed to forget about David Handler for a few minutes. Eventually the sheriff would catch up with Handler and bring him in for questioning. They'd get their information. Until then all they could do was look for Liz.

There seemed to be a million tiny tunnels leading off the main shaft that went through to Yankee Stalwart. Frank and Garth would stand guard in the main shaft while Joe went to investigate a tunnel. Or Joe would watch while Frank went in. Either way, one of them waited in the main shaft to keep an eye out for any more runaway trains.

Three hours later Joe was so tired of breathing in the stale tunnel air, he almost wished he'd brought a can of oxygen. He took the map out of his pocket and scanned the tunnel he and Frank were checking out for any significant markers.

"How much farther do you think it is?" Joe asked, looking up ahead. "Is that the end?"

"You bet it is," Frank said, barely able to hide his frustration.

Frank aimed his flashlight into the darkness. The

bright beam picked up a concrete wall with a thick metal door built into it.

"That must be an entrance to Yankee Stalwart," Frank said.

Joe called out to Garth and told him to come see the wall. When Garth arrived he pounded his fist into the metal door. "And we still haven't found Liz!" he cried in desperation.

"Hold on a minute," Joe said. "There's one last tunnel down here."

Joe pointed his flashlight to the right of the wall, where there was a small tunnel carved into the main shaft.

"It ain't over till it's over," Joe said with a wide grin.

"We'll wait here," Garth said sadly. "I think I've had enough for one night. I can't take getting my hopes up and then being disappointed."

"I'll stay with Garth," Frank said. "You go ahead."

"No problem," Joe said with a shrug.

As he entered the tunnel, Joe saw that it forked off into two more shafts, each one smaller than the main tunnel. He took the fork on the left and quickly came to a dead end. Backing out, he spotted a small chalk mark on the wall separating the two forks.

"That's strange," Joe said, half aloud. He made a note to himself to ask Frank if he'd seen any similar marks on any other tunnels.

117

The second fork went a little deeper into the mine, but not much. Within twenty feet Joe came to another dead end.

"Weird," Joe muttered to himself.

Using his flashlight, Joe scanned the low ceiling and the walls, hoping to find another mark. But there was nothing—no sign that Liz had been there, or that anyone else had been inside the tunnel since the mine closed.

Joe was about to back out of the tunnel when he spotted a tiny crack in the wall on the left. The crack was so small that unless Joe had accidentally shone his flashlight right on it, he never would have noticed it.

He scrambled to look at the crack. Sure enough, if he held the flashlight right up next to it, Joe could see that the crack went all the way through the wall.

"Wait a minute!" Joe cried aloud. "If I can see all the way through, there must be something on the other side—but what?"

Joe stepped back to where the tunnel curved into a fork. On the left was the tunnel where he'd found the mark. On the right was the tunnel where he saw the crack. In front of him Joe was sure he was looking at a solid wall of coal. Or was he?

The ceiling was low, no higher than seven feet. Joe ran his light to the place where the ceiling met the wall. At the top Joe detected another small crack.

"Bingo," he whispered.

Joe could barely contain his excitement. He reached for his penknife, then slowly started working at the crack by the ceiling. Finally, after several tries, he was able to pry loose the coal. An even bigger opening appeared.

"It's a false wall!" Joe shouted. "Frank! Garth! Come here, quick."

There was no answer.

"Frank? Where are you?"

Suddenly Joe got the strange feeling that something had happened to his brother. He left the wall and walked back out to the main shaft.

What Joe saw surprised him even more than the false wall he'd just found.

Frank and Garth were standing by the door that led to Yankee Stalwart. The door was wide open, and Joe saw a man standing by it.

"Frank," Joe said, approaching them.

Frank and Garth stood aside. At that moment Joe was able to make out who the other man was.

It was David Handler!

14 A Strange Twist

"How'd he get here?" Frank heard his brother call out. "What's going on?"

Frank turned around to see Joe covered in coal dust, a penknife in his hand and a scowl on his face.

"Chill out, Joe," Frank said. "David's just finished clearing up some misunderstandings for us."

"Oh, really," Joe said, his eyebrows raised. "Like why he almost ran us down back there? Or why he's been lying to us all along?"

"Now, hold on!" Handler shouted, coming toward Joe. "I'm sick of your accusations."

"Oh, you are, are you?" Joe said. "Well, we're sick of your lies and games."

Handler assumed a defensive karate pose. Luckily, at that moment Garth put his two hundred and fifty pounds between David and Joe. Otherwise, Frank was sure that Handler would have taken more than a few swipes at Joe. He was that mad.

"Hey!" Frank shouted. "Calm down. Both of you."

Joe scowled at Handler over Garth's shoulder. "Why's he our friend all of a sudden? Ten minutes ago we were sure he'd tried to kill us."

Frank held out his hands. "It turns out we had the wrong guy all along."

"Excuse me?" Joe asked skeptically. "Would you care to go over that one again?"

Handler raised his eyebrows. Frank cleared his throat and said, "Dave's not in favor of the proposal. He just pretended that he was."

"So that I could find out what the plan was, from the inside," Handler explained. "And I didn't threaten Liz. In fact, the opposite's true. I wanted to help her out, but she wouldn't let me get involved. My hands were tied!"

"Wait a minute, David." Frank handed Joe a worn, folded piece of paper. "It's Liz's handwriting," he said quietly to his brother. "David just showed it to us."

" 'My dearest David,' " Joe read aloud. " 'I'm on the trail of something big—if only I can get the proof I need, then the people of Ridge City will get the compensation they deserve. I can't tell you more. The less you know, the less you'll have to lie. But please, do one thing for me. Things are pretty

121

hot here, and some powerful people are doing their best to stop me. I'm going to have to disappear, Dave. I need you to make sure no one looks for me. Tell them anything you have to—I died, or went to Australia, whatever. Just keep them off my back for a few days. I know you'll do this for me, and I love you. I promise soon I'll tell you everything. Love, Liz.'"

Joe finished reading and let out a whistle.

"That's why you tried so hard to make us believe Liz had a car accident, isn't it?" Frank asked Handler.

Handler nodded. "I rolled the car over the riverbank myself. I thought that would be the end of it. You can guess how I felt when you guys started insisting that the accident was a fake!"

Garth put a hand on the slender young man's shoulder. "I never believed you meant to hurt her, Dave. I knew you weren't that kind of guy."

"Thanks," Handler said with a little smile. "It's nice to hear that."

"Were you the one who left the flier with Garth's name on it in Liz's desk?" Frank asked.

"Yes. I wanted you to go to the town meeting—I thought you might pick up some clues there."

"Why didn't you just invite us?" Joe growled. "Why the cloak-and-dagger stuff? You could have made all our lives easier if you'd told us what you knew at the beginning."

Handler looked at the ground. "I thought if I stayed away from your investigation, I'd be able to keep my cover better. You know, have the mayor and Adam Brill trust me."

"It makes sense," Frank put in, nodding. "Liz's letter mentions 'powerful people.' She could be talking about the mayor, or Adam Brill—they're both powerful in Ridge City. If David could just stay on their good side, he'd be able to sit in on their meetings and keep an eye out for anything suspicious." He turned to Handler. "Did you find anything?"

Handler shook his head in frustration. "I tried. As far as I can tell, that proposal is fair. The mayor isn't covering anything up. Neither is Yankee Stalwart."

"Except a few accidents," Frank said, half aloud.

"Unfortunately, that's nothing," Handler said. "We all knew about those accidents. They don't affect that proposal. Not a bit. What Liz wanted to find was more proof that Yankee Stalwart had violated regulations somehow. I think she was on to something concrete."

"Like what?" Garth wanted to know.

Handler shook his head slowly. "I wish I could tell you."

"You think that's why she went underground?" Frank asked.

"I think so," Handler said. "When I heard you

and the sheriff were searching the tunnels for her, I decided to look for her myself. I thought at least I might be able to figure out what she was looking for."

"Is this how you got down here?" Garth asked, pointing to the door.

"Yep," Handler said. "I use my passkey to get into Yankee Stalwart, then I came down here through this door."

"But what would Liz be looking for down here?" Frank asked, shrugging his shoulders in confusion.

Just then, Frank saw Joe's eyes grow wide. "Hey!" he cried. "In all the excitement I forgot why I came to get you in the first place. I found something interesting. Come see!"

With that Joe led them back to the place where he'd found the forking tunnels. He showed Frank, Garth, and Handler the space between the tunnel wall and the ceiling.

"So far, that's all I could chip away with my penknife," Joe said. "I wish we had a better tool."

Frank beamed his flashlight into the space. "Someone built this wall," he said. "And made it look like it was just another dead end."

"Exactly," Joe said. "But it's not." He ran his hands over the curving wall. "It goes as far back as that tunnel over there"—Joe pointed to the shaft on the left—"and this one over here." He stretched his hand in the direction of the shaft on the right. "The question is, what's behind here?"

"We'll never find out by chipping away at it with a penknife," Garth said, making a face.

"I've got a solution," Handler said. "Be back in a flash."

Joe watched him go. "I still don't understand why he wrote Liz that threatening note."

"He said he was mad at Liz," Garth explained. "He wanted her to tell him what was going on, but she wouldn't. He said he never had any intention of sending the note."

Handler returned with a couple of pickaxes and some heavy-duty mallets. "This should do it. Compliments of Yankee Stalwart. I just happen to have a key to the toolroom."

"Cool," Frank said. "We'll get this wall down in no time."

The four of them set to tearing down the wall. Ten minutes later they'd chipped away enough of the coal to find out that the wall was really made of chicken wire covered with concrete.

"The coal is just a camouflage," Joe pointed out as he hacked away at the concrete. "Luckily, whoever did this wasn't exactly an expert contractor. Talk about shoddy construction."

Frank managed to dig out a big enough hole in the wall to shine the flashlight through it.

"Wow," he said, peering in. "It looks as if there are about fifteen twenty-gallon barrels in there."

"Of what?" Joe asked.

"I don't know," said Frank. "But I doubt they're

rainwater. Someone went pretty far out of his way to hide them."

Handler scrambled up to the hole and grabbed Frank's flashlight from his hand. He looked in, then turned to Frank with a look of shock and surprise.

"I think we just found a stash of hazardous waste!" Handler cried.

Frank stared at the man. "Are you sure?"

Handler nodded vigorously. "I'm almost positive. Those barrels are the exact ones that the government requires us to use if we dispose of radioactive waste. These aren't marked 'hazardous' or anything, but they must be. Why else would someone hide them like this?"

Frank stepped away from the wall and thought for a moment. "This is serious stuff," he said. "I'll bet you anything Liz had her suspicions about this stash. Maybe she found evidence at Yankee Stalwart about some waste that didn't get disposed of properly."

"Maybe she suspected she'd find it down here," Garth said with excitement.

Frank's thoughts kept racing. "The question is, who hid it? Who has the most to lose if it's found?"

"Adam Brill!" Joe practically shouted.

Handler shook his head. "I don't think so," he said skeptically. "Brill's always seemed honest," he said doubtfully.

"What about those accidents?" Frank asked.

"According to his employees, he's never reported them. In fact," Frank went on slowly, thinking back to the accident he and Joe had witnessed at Yankee Stalwart, "he didn't report that accident just the other day."

"But wouldn't someone have to call the police?" Garth wanted to know. "No matter what?"

"Maybe someone did," Frank said. "Maybe the police know by now not to respond. I didn't hear any sirens, now that I think about it."

"Hold on just a second," Handler said. "What you're saying is that the police are in on this, too? I find that hard to believe."

"Not all the police," Frank said. "But maybe one of them. Sheriff Radford, for example."

"What are you talking about?" Joe demanded. "I thought we ruled Radford out. Now suddenly we've got Brill working with Radford? Where did that come from?"

"Think about it," Frank said, counting off his reasons. "One: If Brill is working with Radford, then it could have been Brill who came to collect the notebook that night at the bridge. Radford could have an accomplice. And Brill's the same size and weight as the guy on the bridge.

"Two: Someone tried to kill us down here tonight. We thought it was Handler, but now we know it wasn't. Who knew where we were?" Frank asked, raising an eyebrow. "Radford."

"And who didn't really bother looking for Liz?" Garth put in. "Remember how it seemed as if he didn't care if he found her or not?"

"And who was out of town the day Liz vanished?" Frank added excitedly. "Sheriff Radford— he was breaking into Garth's apartment that day!"

"But what about the dog hairs?" Joe demanded, looking at his brother in frustration.

Handler put his hand to his chin. "I don't know if this is relevant, but Radford has a dog. I know because I gave him one of my dog's puppies."

"Bingo!" Frank cried, pounding his hand to the wall next to him. "That's enough for me. Look, we need a plan. Obviously, we can't go to Radford for help. We're going to have to contact the FBI. Con Riley can help with that. He's known about this case from the beginning. He'll back us up."

Joe checked his watch. "There's just one problem. It's almost midnight. No FBI agent in the world is going to come out here in the middle of the night because a bunch of kids tell him to."

"True," Frank said, thinking of other options. "Okay. Here's the plan. We go back to Garth's and leave messages for Con—he can contact the FBI. We can call Dad, too, and use him to back us up. We should probably let Mauer know, too. As soon as we get people to believe our story, we head back here."

"Good plan. In the meantime, we lay low, really low," Joe said. "And cross our fingers that Radford

128

or Brill doesn't make any moves until we can stop them."

David Handler came back with the Hardys to spend the night at Garth's house. Frank hardly got any sleep since he was either on the phone all night or waiting for someone to call him back. Finally, at about six in the morning, Con Riley got a promise from two FBI agents to come out to the mines and investigate. Frank had already contacted Fred Mauer. The reporter planned to meet them out at the mines.

The sun was coming up when Garth, Handler, Joe, and Frank got in the van and headed back up to the mines. Frank had given Riley directions for the FBI agents. They were all going to meet at the mine offices.

After Joe had parked the van, they all got out. Frank was restless. He kept thinking about what might have happened to the barrels during the night. Finally he couldn't take the waiting any longer.

"I'm going down there," he said, grabbing a flashlight. "You guys wait up here. You can show the FBI how to get down to where the barrels are hidden."

"No way am I letting you go alone," Joe said. "These guys can stay up here."

"No problem," Garth agreed. "Dave and I will hold down the fort."

129

"Be careful," Frank warned. "Brill or Radford could show up at any moment. They might be armed."

The tunnel that led to Yankee Stalwart seemed endless, but finally Frank and Joe made it there. When Frank rushed into the small, forked tunnel his worst fears were confirmed.

The wall was completely torn down. Smashed concrete lay on the floor, and the chicken wire was cut away. More than half the barrels were gone. There were only seven still there.

"Rats!" Frank kicked the side of the tunnel. "I knew it. One of us should have stayed here last night. This would have never happened."

"Right," Joe said. "Instead, one of us could have been seriously hurt, or worse. If we'd stayed here, Radford or Brill would have made sure we didn't talk about what we saw. Don't worry. There's still at least seven barrels here. That's more than enough proof to nail those guys."

Frank began to cool down. "You're right," he agreed. "What we need to do now is—"

Just then a voice behind them shouted, "Freeze! Don't move, whoever you are!"

15 Runaway Train

"Put your hands in the air and turn around slow, real slow," the voice commanded.

Joe gave Frank a look out of the corner of his eye. The voice sounded as if it belonged to a woman!

"Do it!" demanded the voice. "Now."

"I guess we don't have any choice," Joe said under his breath. "Be prepared for a fast move."

Slowly Joe raised his hands into the air and turned around. He found himself face to face with a small, slender woman dressed in jeans and a black turtleneck. She was holding a pickax. And she looked angry enough to use it.

"Who are you?" the woman demanded, narrowing her eyes and looking at them suspiciously.

"Liz?" Frank guessed. "Are you Liz Trimmer?"

"How do you know my name?" Liz lowered the pickax and looked at them in surprise. "Who are you kids, anyway?"

"We're friends of Garth," Joe told her. He put his hands to his head and exclaimed, "I can't believe we finally found you."

"What do you mean?" Liz asked. Even in the gloom Joe could see her bright blue eyes flashing. "Why were you looking for me?"

Frank laughed out loud. "Why? Only because you disappeared without a trace."

"And because the day after you disappeared, someone sent Garth a ransom note," Joe added.

Liz's eyes went wide with surprise. "Garth thought I was kidnapped!" she cried, obviously stunned.

"You didn't tell anyone where you went," Joe said. "What else were we supposed to think?" He paused and looked Liz over more carefully. She had Garth's sandy blond hair and his piercing blue eyes. Liz was solid muscle, too, but a lot less of it.

She was smiling ruefully. "I wrote Garth a note telling him I was going away," she murmured. "Only I forgot to put it in with the books I sent."

"The kidnapper demanded that Garth return some kind of notebook," Frank said. "He even broke into Garth's apartment, and your house, looking for it."

Liz looked stunned, then angry. She pushed a

loose strand of blond hair behind her ear and reached around to zip open the backpack she wore. She removed a notebook and handed it to Joe.

"That's what your kidnapper was looking for," she said bitterly. "Proof that Adam Brill has spent the past ten years polluting this town."

She gave a scornful laugh. "Here's Brill saying he's voluntarily shutting down the power plant because he's worried about public safety—when the truth is, if the government ever found these barrels of waste, they'd be forced to shut down, and Adam Brill would go to jail! He just wants to close up and get out of Ridge City before anyone catches on."

Joe skimmed through the notebook. A lot of the pages were covered in scientific notations, but there were also daily records of what went on at Yankee Stalwart.

"How did you find this?" Joe asked, handing the notebook to Frank.

Liz smiled and shrugged. Her blue eyes lit up. "I'm a snoop, what else? One of the benefits of working in personnel is you get to take a peek at lots of confidential information. I was looking for evidence that Brill had left a record of the accidents at Yankee Stalwart."

"We heard about those accidents," Frank said. "Did any of them get reported?"

"Not on your life," Liz said. "Brill had Ed

Radford eating out of the palm of his hand. Who knows why, but he did. No one who worked at the plant had the nerve to report the accidents, either. I can't find any proof that the accidents involved radioactive material, but they should have been reported, anyway. I guess the employees were afraid of losing their jobs."

"That makes sense," Joe said. "Especially with the mines closed. Yankee Stalwart was one of the last places to work in Ridge City."

"Exactly," Liz confirmed. "But when I realized that Brill was keeping the accidents a secret—so he wouldn't look incompetent—I started snooping around the plant. That's when I found the notebook, in Brill's office."

"You stole it?" Joe asked.

Liz shook her head. "Not at first. I skimmed through it, didn't find anything. Or so I thought. Then I went back and looked again. That's when I found a notation about hazardous materials, and how Brill was having trouble getting rid of them. He mismanaged funds and couldn't pay to have the waste hauled to a legal dump. I never got a final figure on how many barrels he had to dispose of."

"But you figured he must have hidden them," Frank guessed.

"Right." Liz took a deep breath. "I stole the notebook and decided to search for the barrels. But I didn't think they were down here—there was no sign of them."

"Why did you stay underground for so long?" Joe asked.

"Brill found out that the notebook was gone," Liz said matter-of-factly. "I knew he'd try to come after me for it, once he figured out who took it. It wouldn't take long, since he found me in his office after I read the notebook the first time. Brill isn't stupid. So I disappeared."

"After you sent those other books to Garth," Frank concluded. "Was it Brill who thought you mailed Garth the notebook?"

Liz crossed her arms and said quietly, "No. That was Ed Radford. He ran into me at the post office."

"Whew!" Joe scratched his head and tried to process all the information. "I'm not sure I get all this, but I know one thing. Radford and Brill are trouble. We could be in real danger if they find us down here."

"Especially since it looks as if they were here last night," Frank pointed out. "At least half the barrels that were here yesterday are gone."

Liz walked over to where the chicken wire had been cut away. "I must have searched this area four or five times. I never knew there was a false wall here. How did you figure it out?"

Joe laughed. "I used a secret skill, known only to amateur detectives."

"What's that?" Liz looked quizzical.

"He got lucky!" Frank said, thumping his brother on the back. "That's Joe's favorite method."

Joe scowled, then turned to Liz. "Garth and David Handler are waiting up above. Two FBI agents are supposed to come any minute. Maybe we should go back up? We could all be in danger down here."

"And let Brill and Radford cart off the rest of these barrels?" Liz shook her head emphatically and put her hands on her hips. "No way. I'm staying right here. This is the evidence I've been looking for. This is what will make the government give Ridge City the money it deserves. There are probably countless more of these barrels down here, and that means a thorough investigation and cleanup project."

From the fire in her blue eyes, Joe could tell Liz Trimmer wasn't going to be argued with.

"Okay," Joe agreed. "We'll stay, too."

Liz sat down on the ground beside the torn-down wall. Frank and Joe kept watch by the entrance to the tunnel. Finally in the distance he heard the clattering sound of the train coming down the tunnel.

"They're here!" Joe cried. He turned to face the train while Frank went back inside to collect Liz.

Joe waited expectantly as the train pulled up. The engine car came to a stop, and Joe beamed his flashlight on the people inside.

With a shock Joe realized that it wasn't Garth and Handler who had arrived.

Sheriff Radford and Adam Brill emerged from

the engine car. They both had determined looks on their faces. And they both held guns.

"Nice," Brill said, "very nice. We get two birds at once. Or should I say three?" he added, when Frank emerged with Liz Trimmer. "Get them."

Before Joe could react, Radford had jumped from the train and was coming at Liz and Frank. Liz kicked him hard, landing a blow to the sheriff's knee. Joe rushed into the free-for-all, keeping an eye out for Brill.

Frank and the sheriff were wrestling with each other. Liz circled around them, getting in her kicks. Joe landed a few blows to Radford's stomach, but the sheriff didn't seem to feel them.

Joe was just about to try pulling Frank and the sheriff apart when Frank suddenly fell to the ground in a heap, unconscious.

"What happened? Frank?" Joe stared at his brother, lying on the ground.

Liz tried to wrestle with Radford, but the man was too strong, and soon he had her arms pinned behind her back.

"Don't move," Brill commanded. A nasty expression on his face, he stood behind Frank, with his gun leveled at Joe. "I was forced to knock your brother unconscious. Three against two wasn't fair, anyway."

"You're so right," the sheriff said, keeping his grip tight on Liz.

Brill aimed his gun at Joe. "Get in the train," he

ordered. "Radford, take Liz. We'll tie them up, and then come back for this one. He's not going anywhere."

Joe felt helpless as Brill jabbed the gun into his back and made him get inside the engine car. There were two stools built into the car. Radford tied Liz to one of the stools, then bound Joe to the other. Soon Brill came back and dumped Frank onto the floor of the car. Radford tied Frank's hands and legs together, then roped him to the stool where Liz was tied up.

A moment later Joe heard the sound of something being loaded into the space behind the train.

"The barrels!" Liz said. "They're loading up the rest of the barrels."

Joe felt a knot of fear in his guts. "What's their plan?"

He tried to think quickly. Soon the train would start moving, and their options would be limited. He strained at the ropes, hoping to find some slack. Liz was too far away to be able to help him untie the ropes, so that wasn't an option, and Frank was out cold.

Joe watched as Brill and Radford stepped into the engine car. Radford engaged the gears and slowly reversed the train down the tracks. When they came to the roundabout where all the tunnels converged, Radford turned the train around and set them forward on another track.

"You really know what you're doing," Joe commented. "It seems as if you've been driving around these tunnels quite a bit."

Radford raised his eyebrows. "Maybe."

"Maybe that's why the rails down here are all shiny, like they've been used," Joe said.

Radford turned to stare down at Joe. "Maybe. It could be we've been searching the tunnels for a way to get rid of those barrels."

"Shut up, Radford," Brill warned. "Stop being an idiot. I told you not to tell these punks anything."

After that the two men were silent. Joe kept hoping they'd talk so he might get a sense of their plan. Gradually the tunnel began to smell more and more like sulfur.

"The mine fires," Joe said.

"Where are you taking us?" Liz demanded.

Brill sneered down at them. "Radford and I have done some investigating of our own. We've learned that the tunnel we're in goes straight into a shaft that's on fire. Unfortunately, you three are going to have a terrible accident."

"You're going to let us crash into one of the fires," Joe guessed, horrified.

"Precisely," Brill commented.

"What about the barrels?" Liz asked. "You can't hide those."

"We think the fire will pretty much destroy everything," Radford said. "I don't know why we didn't think of letting the mine fires burn up those barrels earlier—"

Liz gasped. "But that stuff is toxic! Who knows what it'll do to the environment?"

"Enough chitchat," Brill told Radford. "Pull the throttle and let's go."

Joe stretched against the ropes, hoping to see what the sheriff was doing. The train raced forward. As far as Joe could tell, Radford was tying the engine throttle so that the train would go speeding into the tunnel. There was no way they would be able to knock the throttle or shut it off if it was tied in place. Then Joe heard the sound of glass breaking, and Radford and Brill stepped off to the side of the train. "So long, chums!" Brill called out. "Have a nice trip."

"What are we going to do?" Liz cried out.

The train gained speed. Up ahead Joe could see the smoke and dancing flames of a mine fire burning. The air became choked with sulfur. Liz gasped. Joe felt his throat clench. Next to them Frank still lay unconscious.

The flames came closer. The train went faster and faster. It was no use. They were going to explode in the fire!

16 The Great Escape

Joe strained at the ropes that bound him to the stool. If only he were close enough to Liz, maybe she could untie them with her own hands. There had to be a way.

At that moment Joe spotted his brother moving on the ground next to him.

"Frank!" Joe cried out. "Wake up. We're in trouble. Frank!"

Frank Hardy struggled to open his eyes. He shook his head several times. Finally he was able to keep his eyes open.

"What's happening?" Frank mumbled. "Where are we? Something's on fire."

"You bet something's on fire," Joe confirmed.

"And unless we do something, pretty soon *we're* going to be on fire! We've got a few minutes before this thing blows," Joe said, trying to keep calm.

Frank sat up and peered at the control panel, rapidly assessing the situation. "We need a plan, and fast," he confirmed.

Joe looked around the engine car, hoping that there was some kind of tool that might help them out. In a far corner of the engine car he spotted a pickax. "Liz!" he cried. "Can you reach that ax?"

Liz stretched out her legs and tried to grab it with her feet. "It's no good," she said. "I'm not tall enough. You try," she urged Frank.

Frank maneuvered his legs as close as possible to the ax, but he couldn't reach it, either. "I'm too far away," he said. "You're closer, Liz. Come on, try again."

Liz struggled to get as much slack as she could out of the ropes that held her hands to the stool. She stretched her legs toward the back corner of the car. Finally Joe heard her toe make contact with the ax.

"You've got it!" Joe cried. "Now just drag it back. Slow. Come on. Easy now. All right!"

Liz pulled her legs up and grabbed the ax handle from between her feet.

"Turn around," Liz said to Frank. "Put your back to me. I'll try to loosen the ropes. Maybe we can get enough slack in there for you to get your hands out."

Joe tried not to notice how close they were getting to the fire. There was hardly any time.

"That's it!" Frank called out, pulling his hands around in front of him and reaching down to loosen the rope around his feet. "Give me the pickax," he said.

Frank took the tool from Liz and quickly pried loose the ropes around Liz's hands. Then the two of them got Joe free. Seconds later Frank, Joe, and Liz were standing at the engine car's control panel.

"There's still just one problem," Joe said. "The control panel's broken. Brill and Radford smashed it before they jumped off. Even if we get this throttle back to normal, we may not be able to stop the train."

"We've got to try," Liz said in desperation. "This fire is getting hotter every second. We're going to burn up."

Joe quickly untied the throttle and pulled it back all the way. The train slowed considerably. But Joe knew unless they managed to switch it to "off," they were still in danger.

"That gives us some time," Frank said.

"A little," Joe agreed. He peered underneath the control panel. There were several wires hanging down, loose. "If we can figure out which of these wires runs the train's electricity, we can switch it off."

"Try these." Frank held up a red wire and a black wire that were held together by a fuse.

143

Joe yanked on the wires. The fuse broke open, and the wires came apart. But the train kept speeding down the tracks.

"No good," Joe muttered tensely.

"How about these?" Liz asked. She pulled a yellow wire and a blue wire out from underneath the control panel.

Before Joe could reach for the wires, Liz had them apart. Suddenly, with a terrible screeching sound, the train jolted to a stop.

"All right!" Joe cried, giving Liz a high five. "Way to go."

Frank slapped Liz on the back. "Trimmer to the rescue!" he joked. "Wait till Garth hears."

Liz smiled with exhaustion and relief. "Garth's used to my being a hero," she said, laughing.

Joe, meanwhile, was still fumbling with the wires. He tried a few connections and finally found what he was looking for. The train rumbled alive, and started backing out through the tunnel.

Frank looked at his brother in surprise. "Since when did you become an electronics expert?" he asked.

Joe laughed. "Since a second ago." He moved the throttle forward, and the train picked up speed. "I thought we could back out of this tunnel and hunt down Radford and Brill."

"Excellent," Liz said, beaming. "This time they really will be outnumbered."

"Remember what they say," Frank warned. "It ain't over till it's over."

Joe managed to reverse the train back through the tunnel. "Which way do you think they went?" he asked when they came to the roundabout where all the tunnels met.

In answer Frank pointed to two figures at the entrance to the tunnel that led back to Yankee Stalwart. "There!" he cried. "Can you get the train to go forward?"

"Hurry," Liz urged. "They're getting away."

In the darkness the train's beam picked up Brill and Radford running along the tracks. Joe untwisted the wires on the control panel, switched them, and twisted them back again.

"Here goes," Joe said, pushing the throttle forward.

The train lurched ahead.

"Way to go!" Frank cried out. "Let's get 'em."

Joe's heart was thundering in his chest. From the moment they'd escaped the fire and managed to get the train moving back out of the tunnel, Joe had felt his adrenaline surging. Now his body tingled with tension as the train picked up speed toward Brill and Radford.

The two men figured out that they were being followed and tried to run even faster. But it was too late. The train quickly overtook them.

"Watch out," Frank warned. Radford and Brill

peeled away from the path of the train and pressed themselves against the tunnel wall. "Don't let them get away."

Without wasting another moment Joe leapt from the train. Radford was on the left hand side of the tunnel. Joe took off after him.

"You guys cover Brill!" Joe cried to Frank and Liz as he raced for the sheriff.

Up ahead, Radford lumbered down the tunnel. It was an easy job to catch up with him. Joe was hardly out of breath when he jumped onto Radford's back and tackled the man to the ground.

The sheriff tried to put up a fight, but Joe was too strong. One blow to the man's jaw was enough to convince Radford that he was outmanned.

"I give up!" the sheriff cried, holding his hands in front of his face. "Don't hurt me."

"Don't be a jerk," Joe said, pulling the man to his feet. "Give me those cuffs."

Joe took the sheriff's handcuffs from him and locked Radford's wrists into them.

"You need any help back there?" Joe heard Frank call out down the tunnel.

"No, thanks," Joe said. "Did you get Brill?"

"You bet," came Liz's voice. "He still doesn't know what hit him."

"You've got some serious explaining to do," Joe said as he led the sheriff back to where Frank and Liz were holding down Brill. "Both of you."

* * *

146

Three hours later everyone met in Mayor Stephenson's office. Frank and Joe were there, along with Garth, Liz, Handler, Angela, Fred Mauer, and the two FBI agents. Jackie George was busily taking notes on what Frank, Joe, and Liz were explaining to her about the accidents at Yankee Stalwart. Liz had already told her about the notebook and the barrels of waste. Liz also explained how her suspicions had made her go underground to find evidence of Brill's wrongdoing.

"I just can't believe all this," Jackie said, her warm brown eyes wide with surprise. "I've worked with Adam Brill for three months. I would never have suspected him. Not at all. To think that even employees didn't feel comfortable about coming forward."

"I think it's an example of one mistake creating another," Handler offered. "Brill was afraid to report the first accident to the police or his shareholders."

"But Radford found out," Joe said.

"And turned it to his advantage," Frank said. "Apparently Adam Brill was paying the sheriff off and making him do his dirty work. That included breaking into Garth's apartment and sending him that note. The sheriff also admits to ransacking the Trimmer house. He was still looking for that notebook Liz took from Yankee Stalwart."

"It's just terrible for our town to have this happen," the mayor said sadly.

147

"As far as we can tell," Liz went on, "after that first accident Brill and Radford worked together to hide any mismanagement at Yankee Stalwart. Every time there was an accident, Radford helped hush it up—luckily, none of them was radioactive. Radford also knew about the illegal dumping that Brill was guilty of. Brill had a couple of his employees helping him dispose of the barrels."

"It's incredible," Mayor Stephenson said, obviously in shock. She blinked several times. "To think this was going on right under my nose."

"So Liz was right all along," Angela Golding said proudly. "You suspected this town deserved more help from the government," she said to Liz. "No one appreciated what you were doing."

"That's because as usual my sister was about as stubborn as they come," Garth said, putting an arm around Liz.

Mayor Stephenson got up from her desk and went around to where Liz and Garth sat on the couch. David Handler was on the other side of Liz, holding her hand.

"I hate to admit when I'm wrong," the mayor said. She reached out to shake Liz's hand. "But in this case, I was—and I'm glad you were here to show me."

"So it was also Radford who tried to mow us down with the train," Joe said after a while.

"You bet it was," Frank agreed. "He set us up by telling us to search that particular tunnel. The sheriff could have had a job moonlighting as a conductor, he was so good at driving that train."

Fred Mauer stood up and stretched out his back. "I've got to file this story in ten minutes or else I'll miss my deadline. Is there anything else I should know?"

Jackie George spoke up. "Just that the government is prepared to revise its proposal now that we know about the dumping at the mines. There will be an investigation to find out just how many barrels are hidden down there. The groundwater around here will need to be tested, as well as the reservoir, and those barrels have to be disposed of properly. Ridge City is going to get a lot more money."

"How much more?" Liz piped up.

Mayor Stephenson shot Liz a serious look. "Still the troublemaker, I see."

With that Garth hugged Liz closer to him and said, "Some things never change. Especially not in Ridge City."

"So, Garth," Joe asked, giving his friend a wry smile. "Do you still think this town stinks?"

Garth wrinkled his nose. "I guess not. Actually, thanks to Liz, Ridge City is smelling better and better every day!"

THE HARDY BOYS® SERIES By Franklin W. Dixon

☐ #59: NIGHT OF THE WEREWOLF	70993-3/$3.50	
☐ #60: MYSTERY OF THE SAMURAI		
SWORD	67302-5/$3.99	
☐ #61: THE PENTAGON SPY	67221-5/$3.99	
☐ #62: THE APEMAN'S SECRET	69068-X/$3.50	
☐ #63: THE MUMMY CASE	64289-8/$3.99	
☐ #64: MYSTERY OF SMUGGLERS COVE	66229-5/$3.50	
☐ #65: THE STONE IDOL	69402-2/$3.50	
☐ #66: THE VANISHING THIEVES	63890-4/$3.99	
☐ #67: THE OUTLAW'S SILVER	74229-9/$3.50	
☐ #68: DEADLY CHASE	62477-6/$3.50	
☐ #69: THE FOUR-HEADED DRAGON	65797-6/$3.50	
☐ #70: THE INFINITY CLUE	69154-6/$3.50	
☐ #71: TRACK OF THE ZOMBIE	62623-X/$3.50	
☐ #72: THE VOODOO PLOT	64287-1/$3.99	
☐ #73: THE BILLION DOLLAR		
RANSOM	66228-7/$3.50	
☐ #74: TIC-TAC TERROR	66858-7/$3.50	
☐ #75: TRAPPED AT SEA	64290-1/$3.50	
☐ #76: GAME PLAN FOR DISASTER	72321-9/$3.50	
☐ #77: THE CRIMSON FLAME	64286-3/$3.99	
☐ #78: CAVE IN	69486-3/$3.50	
☐ #79: SKY SABOTAGE	62625-6/$3.50	
☐ #80: THE ROARING RIVER		
MYSTERY	73004-5/$3.50	
☐ #81: THE DEMON'S DEN	62622-1/$3.50	
☐ #82: THE BLACKWING PUZZLE	70472-9/$3.50	
☐ #83: THE SWAMP MONSTER	49727-8/$3.50	
☐ #84: REVENGE OF THE DESERT		
PHANTOM	49729-4/$3.50	
☐ #85: SKYFIRE PUZZLE	67458-7/$3.50	
☐ #86: THE MYSTERY OF THE		
SILVER STAR	64374-6/$3.50	
☐ #87: PROGRAM FOR DESTRUCTION	64895-0/$3.99	
☐ #88: TRICKY BUSINESS	64973-6/$3.99	
☐ #89: THE SKY BLUE FRAME	64974-4/$3.50	
☐ #90: DANGER ON THE DIAMOND	63425-9/$3.99	

☐ #91: SHIELD OF FEAR	66308-9/$3.50
☐ #92: THE SHADOW KILLERS	66309-7/$3.99
☐ #93: THE SEPENT'S TOOTH	
MYSTERY	66310-0/$3.50
☐ #94: BREAKDOWN IN AXEBLADE	66311-9/$3.50
☐ #95: DANGER ON THE AIR	66305-4/$3.50
☐ #96: WIPEOUT	66306-2/$3.50
☐ #97: CAST OF CRIMINALS	66307-0/$3.50
☐ #98: SPARK OF SUSPICION	66304-6/$3.99
☐ #99: DUNGEON OF DOOM	69449-9/$3.50
☐ #100: THE SECRET OF ISLAND	
TREASURE	69450-2/$3.50
☐ #101: THE MONEY HUNT	69451-0/$3.50
☐ #102: TERMINAL SHOCK	69288-7/$3.50
☐ #103: THE MILLION-DOLLAR	
NIGHTMARE	69272-0/$3.99
☐ #104: TRICKS OF THE TRADE	69273-9/$3.50
☐ #105: THE SMOKE SCREEN	
MYSTERY	69274-7/$3.99
☐ #106: ATTACK OF THE	
VIDEO VILLIANS	69275-5/$3.99
☐ #107: PANIC ON GULL ISLAND	69276-3/$3.99
☐ #108: FEAR ON WHEELS	69277-1/$3.99
☐ #109: THE PRIME-TIME CRIME	69278-X/$3.50
☐ #110: THE SECRET OF SIGMA SEVEN	72717-6/$3.99
☐ #111: THREE-RING TERROR	73057-6/$3.99
☐ #112: THE DEMOLITION MISSION	73058-4/$3.99
☐ #113: RADICAL MOVES	73060-6/$3.99
☐ #114: THE CASE OF THE	
COUNTERFEIT CRIMINALS	73061-4/$3.50
☐ #115: SABOTAGE AT SPORTS CITY	73062-2/$3.99
☐ #116: ROCK 'N' ROLL RENEGADES	73063-0/$3.99
☐ #117: THE BASEBALL CARD CONSPIRACY	73064-9/$3.99
☐ #118: DANGER IN THE FOURTH DIMENSION	79308-X/$3.99
☐ #119: TROUBLE AT COYOTE CANYON	79309-8/$3.99
☐ #120: CASE OF THE COSMIC KIDNAPPING	79310-1/$3.99
☐ THE HARDY BOYS GHOST STORIES	69133-3/$3.50

Simon & Schuster, Mail Order Dept. HB5, 200 Old Tappan Rd., Old Tappan, N.J. 07675
Please send me copies of the books checked. Please add appropriate local sales tax.

☐ Enclosed full amount per copy with this coupon (Send check or money order only)

☐ If order is $10.00 or more, you may charge to one of the following accounts: ☐ Mastercard ☐ Visa
Please be sure to include proper postage and handling: 0.95 for first copy; 0.50 for each additional copy ordered.

Name _____

Address _____

City _____ State/Zip _____

Credit Card # _____ Exp.Date _____

Signature _____

Books listed are also available at your bookstore. Prices are subject to change without notice.   657-03

NANCY DREW® MYSTERY STORIES By Carolyn Keene